River of Secrets

RIVER OF SECRETS

by

FOZA HILAL

In "River of Secrets," the protagonist, Farah, brings attention to the struggles Syrians faced in a decade-long conflict that devastated their lives. Born out of wedlock, abandoned, and orphaned, Farah was taken in by a kind-hearted family but later grew up feeling lost due to her unknown lineage. She never attended school and became aware of her social standing only when she experienced humiliation and degradation in various circumstances.

Finding solace in work, Farah served as a housekeeper for several families and, through this occupation, gained insight into the moral fabric of diverse social groups. The novel delves into how the turmoil within the country shaped people's actions and how their behavior affected Farah, leaving scars that time couldn't heal. Refusing to yield to her fate, Farah's unwavering determination kept her true to herself as she persevered through adversity, symbolizing patience and resilience.

The novel was revised and translated through a collaboration between the author Foza Hilal and the translation department at Khayat Publishing House. Additionally, both internal and external designs for the novel were created by the design team at Khayat.

RIVER OF SECRETS

First published in 2024

ISBN: 978-1-961420-99-1

Copyright © Foza Hilal 2024

Library of Congress Control Number: 2024934126

KHAYAT

WASHINGTON, DC
UNITED STATES

www.khayatpublishing.com

FOZA HILAL

River Of Secrets

Blossoming out of ashes!

CHAPTER 1

Exhausted from work, I returned home and threw my head onto a pillow that felt like thorns, pricking me. Sleep eluded me, as troubling thoughts clung to my mind. How did I come into this world? What crime did I commit to live this way? How did I survive the war and rubble that engulfed both Um Bassam's mother and me?

She opened her home and treated me like a daughter. No mother showered me with warmth, and no father supported me. Now, I lost her.

I peered through the window, gazing at the moonlit sky. I envied the moon for the radiant stars surrounding it. I lay alone in my dark room. Anxiety and fatigue overwhelmed me, as memories of a painful past resurfaced along with the mysteries of an uncertain future. I loved my homeland but owned nothing but my name. I possessed no identification card to prove who I was. No one acknowledged my existence.

I was indebted to Um Bassam for teaching me how to write my name and furthering my education until my literacy became acceptable. She had stood by me since childhood. She fought with her husband over registering me under their family name. He disagreed, fearing that one day my true nature would be revealed because of my roots.

I remembered when Um Bassam whispering to neighbors, telling them Um Farah might be exposed as a dishonorable girl. She had heard rumors about my mother Um Fidda being involved with a young man from outside town. My mother's father, the chicken seller Abi Riya, threatened to kill her. She fled to the house of her sister, who lived alone because her husband was abroad.

I had heard this story ever since I was little, until fate took Um Bassam's life. I then came to this town hoping to learn about my mother. I only knew Mulham, a young man. I hid my true identity, fearing my secret would be exposed and no one would trust me. I told Mulham my parents and family had died when our home was destroyed in the war. I said I'd barely survived, and he cared for me. Mulham searched for a house to shelter me and found me a job. He introduced me to the household of Um Sadiq, where I work now.

I dozed from sheer exhaustion, but slept restlessly. In nightmares, voices of my employers commanded me.

Um Sadiq: "Don't forget to feed the dogs!"

Bu Sadiq: "Iron the clothes!"

Um Adham: "Clean the stairs!"

Um Khaled: "Hang the laundry!"

I didn't know where to begin. My God, fatigue followed me even when I closed my eyes.

I woke to the sounds of birds, chickens, and cats coming from the neighbor's garden, which was filled with trees whose branches shaded my bedroom window. The birds caught my attention as they moved among branches. They lived in freedom, not waiting for orders from anyone. Some carried straw in their beaks to build a safe nest. Others brought food for their babies, calling with a distinct voice as they hurried after them. Others joyfully chirped.

One morning, I was moved by the sight of a cat carrying her kitten in her teeth, fleeing from the violent tomcat trying to devour her offspring. This scene reminded me of what Um Bassam told me when she found me in front of the mosque and took me to her house to care for me.

I wished she had left me for the wild beasts to devour; instead, I lived in a society that didn't understand me, a society that blamed me for just being myself, a society that didn't know I had nothing to do with the sins of those who brought me into this world. I wanted to call to the mother I never knew, hoping she might hear my voice: Why did you bring me into this world?

I was in neither the place nor the time to rise above. I wished for a nest where I could seek refuge and live peacefully. For all I possessed in this world was my dignity—a dignity no one acknowledged.

After getting lost in these thoughts, I realized it was time for work, and had no time for breakfast. My thoughts wandered to Um Sadiq's dogs and birds, which might have been hungrier than me.

***

CHAPTER 2

Shortly before I reached Um Sadiq's house, I was surprised by her dogs heading toward me, their barking a language of reproach because I was so late. I blamed myself for not learning to stick to schedules or being taught the importance of time management and organization. Everyone around me lived in chaos.

Immediately, I fed them. As they devoured their food, they looked at me as if grateful. Loyalty was one of their traits—unlike some people. Um Sadiq's birds were also waiting for their food, their chirping growing louder from hunger. I served them as well, understanding their suffering. Sometimes, I'd talk to them as if they could understand me, too.

"Why are you imprisoned in cages, birds? Are you being punished for a crime? Anyone who puts you in a cage is sorely mistaken!"

After finishing my work in the garden, I entered the house, and Um Sadiq's daughter shouted in my face, "The maid has arrived!"

I wished they would call me by my name "Farah," which Um Bassam gave me.

I hated the words "maid" or "servant" being attached to me. Sometimes, I'd forget my own name. I had no choice but to avoid the family by staying in the kitchen. I knew after they finished breakfast, I'd be faced with washing the dishes and pots, not knowing where to start amid the clattering of pots. Um Sadiq called me and asked for their morning coffee. I served them and heard their whispers after returning to the kitchen. A woman, Um Sadiq's friend, said: "What a beautiful maid! How did you find her?"

"Through one of my husband's friends!" said Um Sadiq.

"How do you accept such a beautiful girl in your house?" said the friend. "Don't you feel jealous your husband's attention will wander? Beauty excites all men."

"She is different from others. She wouldn't allow anyone to cross boundaries or get too familiar with her. She works hard and speaks seriously without meddling in anything that doesn't concern her."

Um Sadiq's friend was surprised that someone like me, with such physical attributes, worked as a maid.

"I'm curious to get to know her," the friend said.

I expected Um Sadiq's friend to ask me why I did this work; if I answered truthfully, I could lose my livelihood. I was surprised Um Sadiq had never asked for details about me.

"Farah, come here," Um Sadiq called.

I was happy to hear my name and stood before them.

"Um Adham would like to get to know you," she said.

"Are you from this village?" Um Adham asked.

I replied that I wasn't from this village or province before Um Sadiq interrupted.

"It's enough for me to trust the young man who sent her to us," Um Sadiq said.

"He is one of our close relatives."

I stood like a soldier waiting for orders. My legs trembled with fear as I endured her questioning when, suddenly, the dog rushed in sniffing around Um Adham as if informing her of something.

After hearing Um Adham's husband call from behind the fence, it became clear they were neighbors. Before leaving, Um Adham said to Um Sadiq, "When I need her help, I will let you know and you can send Farah to help me."

Um Sadiq reassured her I was good at domestic work and skilled in cooking. After her friend left, Um Sadiq took a deep breath.

"Finally, we got rid of her. Sometimes we must sit with people who are imposed on us and have to go along with them, listen to them, and pretend to care. It's two in the afternoon, and she's been chattering away non-stop."

Nothing Um Sadiq said entered my ears because I didn't care. I kept my opinions to myself about what I saw and heard because society demanded it. I responded only when asked. I looked forward to the end of my workday so I could return home. There, I shared my opinions with myself and spoke freely whenever I pleased.

Um Sadiq asked me to prepare the dining table. It was time for her husband Bu Sadiq to come home; I'd learned he was an army officer.

Feeling bold, I told her the army was on high alert, so he might not be able to come home.

"I have spoken to him and asked him to bring lunch with him," she said.

Just as she finished speaking, the doorbell rang. Bu Sadiq entered carrying what his wife had requested. The dog greeted him excitedly because it smelled the meat he'd brought. The dog hurried to take a seat at the table like a family member. When I quickly removed him, the little girl Ameera shouted, "Let him eat with us!"

I wished I could be like this dog, having someone who cares for me, treasures me, and loves me. I returned to the kitchen to wait for their meal to end so that my day of troubles and stress would finally end as well. Then I heard Bu Sadiq call me: "Take your portion of the food. Today you will stay with us. I invited my fellow officers to come over in the evening for dinner and drinks. We might need you."

I thought about taking a nap after the family members went to sleep in their rooms. I sat on a chair in the kitchen, listening to the faint sound of the news on the radio, so as not to disturb anyone. The news was not good: the army was on high alert because of rampant terrorism across the country. There were bombings here, suicide bombers there, and widespread kidnappings everywhere. Nothing was comforting. I wondered how this did not bother some people, who seemed to only care about eating and drinking.

I began chopping parsley and preparing tab-bouleh for the evening party. When Um Sadiq and her husband woke, I heard her voice rise against her husband.

"I don't like these parties and don't want them," she said. "They cause disturbances. You are in a sensitive government position. You should not have parties like this one. The neighborhood gets annoyed by your noise. It's better to call your friends and cancel this party."

He asked in surprise, "How can I cancel it when it's my turn to host the dinner?"

"It wouldn't be the end of the world if you canceled it!"

"Have you lost your mind, woman?"

"I don't like these empty late-night gatherings!"

"And I don't appreciate your trivial opinions!"

"So, I'm trivial to you now? Time will tell who's trivial among us!"

He interrupted angrily, "The gathering will go on, whether you like it or not."

She cut him off, "Now you're resorting to threats?"

He raised his voice in irritation. "I am the man of this house. My word will be followed, and I won't repeat myself. If you don't like it, go hit your head against the wall!"

"There's no use arguing with you. You know what? I tolerate you for the sake of our children, so they don't live without a father, even though they imitate your unbearable behaviors."

He left, slamming the door of the room angrily and murmuring on his way to meet colleagues. She didn't leave the room, her anger clearly visible. She vented frustration by yelling at the children, even though they were playing silently.

After preparing everything for their gathering, I returned to my seat in the kitchen and waited for instructions. I felt I might collapse in a heap from exhaustion.

The officers' voices grew louder as they played cards and clinked glasses. Their voices intensified with enthusiasm and happiness when one of them won a round. I despised that game and loathed the unbearable chatter of the players. I waited for the gathering to end so I could finally relax.

I fell asleep in my chair, and awakened to the sound of a creaking door as someone left. I thought to myself: "Finally, some relief. They are leaving!" Suddenly, a gunshot rang out. My God! What just happened? The atmosphere was tense and frightening, with everyone excited and noise coming from all sides. It turned out someone was celebrating his victory in the game by firing his pistol.

Honestly, May God help you, Um Sadiq! Is this kind of behavior reasonable in the middle of the night? And scaring innocent children like this?

The phone rang. Um Sadiq yelled to me, "Answer the phone!" The neighbors anxiously inquired about the gunshot. I hesitated, uncertain how to answer. I finally said:

"They're expressing their joyful victory."

"Joy for what? Did they defeat the rebels?" the neighbor said.

"No, Bu Sadiq won a card game!"

"What a shame at his rank. People are worried about the war, and he's oblivious. May God help Um Sadiq deal with him. He's always ruining her life with his childish behavior."

She began cursing before hanging up. Um Sadiq quickly gathered her family's clothes in a suitcase.

"You won't see my face again until we're in court," she said to her husband.

However, the alcohol had taken effect and put him to sleep. His snoring reached the end of the street.

Then, she called me to get ready to go with them to her parents' house; she'd decided never to return. How can you leave after midnight? I thought. The road isn't safe.

"I called my brother and he's coming to pick us up," she said.

The children shouted in glee: "Hurrayyy! We're going to grandma's house!"

**

CHAPTER 3

Sleep won't come until I jot down the thoughts I can only confide in my diary; like when Bu Sadiq lied to his wife, telling her that he was going on a mission when I'd heard him telling his girlfriend how they could meet at the Blue Beach. Once, he even tried to convince me to join him so he could introduce me to his friend, enticing me with money and a glimpse of the sea. Of course, money was everything in his life; he traded the blood of patriots for money, selling all his comrades stationed in tents to protect the nation.

Um Sadiq bore all his flaws and defended him, but her countenance could not hide that she cared about her children first and foremost. Yet if she were to officially separate from he husband she feared what her parents and community would say. She told her friend Sana that society is unforgiving, "They always blame us, the women; we must live like this our entire lives, as divorce is a disgrace."

Sana told her to be grateful. "Those who live like you are envied by others—a palace, a car, a maid, and your children in private schools, you lack nothing. But we struggle to cover our rent."

Um Sadiq sighed and stayed silent at first.

"Money, house, car, and maid don't make a home happy. You're happy when you put your head on the pillow with a clear conscience," she finally said.

"Dear Um Sadiq, what's wrong with you?" Sana said.

"Oh Sana, I cannot sleep at night and my conscience torments me. How am I still living with this man? I won't hide it from you; I can't stand it anymore. Imagine what I'm about to tell you: I learned that my husband takes the monthly salaries of soldiers in exchange for sending them home on leave while our country is in this delicate situation. Whoever betrays his country will betray his wife and cannot be trusted with anything."

After listening, Sana couldn't help but express her thoughts.

"My friend, for a long time, I've heard the neighbors talking about him. He takes bribes left and right. Haven't you ever doubted him or asked where all this wealth comes from? My husband has the same rank yet we live just on his salary and are quite happy. Your husband has a weak soul that worships money!"

I listened as I stood in the kitchen amidst the clanking dishes. I could hear clearly because the kitchen was partly open to the guest room. Um Sadiq and her husband both trusted me with their secrets because they thought I was either foolish or oblivious to what I heard.

Now, I felt helpless because I was aware of his previous betrayal of his wife and the crime he committed, which went unpunished because of his high rank and government corruption. If she knew this, she would go mad. I was happy when Um Sadiq finally separated from her husband. She could live a life that suits her conscience. As for me, though, their separation meant leaving Um Sadiq's house. I had to secure a livelihood elsewhere. I spent days searching without a lead.

To my surprise, Bu Sadiq called me one day.

"Farah, Um Sadiq is sick," he said. "You have to come and help her."

He hung up before I could ask questions. I was puzzled because I thought Um Sadiq was living with her family after I'd left. I was worried about her and wondered if she had changed her mind. I had doubts about what her husband said, though. I called Um Sadiq several times to make sure she'd returned to Bu Sadiq. When she didn't answer, my concern grew.

I decided to honor Bu Sadiq's request by going to his house. Eager to know about Um Sadiq, my heart raced as I rang the doorbell. Bu Sadiq opened the door with a cheerful face and a wide smile. I stood outside the door. When I asked about Um Sadiq, he didn't answer.

Upon entering, I felt a sense of gloom. Where were the flowers that used to cover the walls? Yellow, wilted leaves had fallen and were scattered here and there. Where were the birds with joyful songs that delighted the neighbors? They lay dead inside their cages. Where were the loyal dogs, barking to greet me no matter how late I'd arrived? The house seemed devoid of life.

I was certain Um Sadiq had not returned.

After I entered, Bu Sadiq pulled me farther inside by my hand. Hurrying, he locked the door from within and stuck the key in his jacket pocket. His behavior and sinister glances terrified me.

I repeated my question about Um Sadiq. He grew bolder and blurted: "You are now Um Sadiq's replacement. We separated since she left for her parents' house."

I pushed him angrily and spoke loudly.

"You are a despicable, liar of a man! You tell me she is ill, you wretch?"

He merely absorbed the insult and responded in a simmering voice.

"I love you!" he said.

"I hated you from the first day I entered your house," I said. "I came out of respect for Um Sadiq's dignity. I know you are a thief and a troublemaker, and I know you were cheating on your wife."

My harsh words hurt him, so he took off his jacket and sat on a chair next to the door. I remained standing and pounded my fist on the door forcefully. I hoped he would open it or one of the neighbors would hear the commotion and rescue me from this scoundrel.

He spoke calmly.

"I called you to come clean the house," he said.

Then he turned toward the closet. He retrieved a bundle of money. When he handed it to me, I threw it in his face. I screamed for him to open the door so I could leave.

His anger flared, eyes turning red and focusing on me like a predator. In his rage, he couldn't find the key. I reminded him it was in his jacket pocket. I spat on him while I fled and he yelled.

"I damn you to hell, Farah!"

On the street, I told myself he deserved this life, in a house now reeking of filth and decay. He didn't deserve a faithful woman like Um Sadiq. His end would be dismal.

Still, I wondered: Why do people mock me and try to break me when I work in their homes? With all they have, they could instead be helping me improve my situation.

On such an exhausting night, I awaited the sun's rays to refresh hope.

***

CHAPTER 4

I walked the streets without knowing where I was going, whom I would talk to, or where to find a job. My first time exploring this town, I looked left and right. I found myself near a park. Entering, I noticed people gathered in groups and by themselves in joy. Seeing people of different backgrounds and beliefs come together as a beautiful, unified tapestry warmed my heart.

Still, I sat on a bench alone with my sadness. I suffered from an open, bleeding wound. I saw love and passion in everyone's eyes, along with hope. Through them, I perceived what I lacked—love, affection, and closeness. I had no family, relatives, or friends. I wished to know some of the people in the park, even become friends. However, along with these wishes, I feared them discovering the details of my origins. I'd learned to admit my mistakes. Yet that mistake was not mine, but instead, those who brought me into this world.

I strolled among the park's trees and flowers to expunge the negative energy caused by Bu Sadiq, who thought he could buy anything with money from fraud and deception. I left the park and headed home to rest. I hoped to see Mulham again, as I believed he was the only one who could help me secure a job.

Before entering my house, I read a note on the door: "I'll be back tomorrow." Surprised, I found no name. I wondered who could have left it since nobody entered our house. I suspected it could be my neighbor Suad from next door. Or, maybe she knew about this mysterious note. When I asked, she replied sarcastically, "Am I the guardian of the door to your house?" before slamming her door.

Saddened, I returned and threw myself onto the bed. The world spun. I remembered the dear Um Bassam who raised me. When she made stuffed zucchini, kibbeh, or other dishes, she'd send me to share her food with neighbors. How life had changed. War had brought misery to all.

Ideally, in times of crisis and war, people increase their cooperation and love for one another. Yet here, neighbors no longer recognized each other. Or, perhaps my neighbor disrespected me for working in other people's homes. It didn't matter. The important thing was that I lived by the sweat of my brow and didn't burden anyone.

I heard the squeak of Suad's door opening. Then, light knocks on my door.

"It's your neighbor Suad, open for me."

Suad entered with a radiant face after her anger had faded. She'd realized her mistake and greeted me with a smile.

"Please come in," I said warmly.

Before she offered any pleasantries, she began apologizing.

"What's wrong, Suad?" I asked.

"For nine years, I have taken responsibility for five children while my husband works abroad. Today, I woke up happy after I heard from him that he was coming back from his trip. However, a disaster occurred. My husband was kidnapped upon arriving in the country. He and his driver were taken from the airport, and no one knows where they are now. I'm confused and don't know what to do; I've been angry and tense since hearing."

"Oh Suad," I said. "God willing, he will return to you safe and sound. I'm not upset with you. You are like a sister to me. If you need anything that I can help with, just let me know, and I won't hesitate."

—

"I'd like you to come and spend the night at my house. I am alone with my children in this town. I have no relatives here. Up to now, I still do not know your name."

"My name is Farah."

"All right, I'll be waiting for you, Farah. I'm going now. After serving dinner to the children and putting them to bed, I will call for you."

"Inshallah," I said.

After she left, I worried she'd ask about the details of my life. Should I deny the truth like I did with Mulham? But my conscience still bothered me about that. Should I be honest with her? I was now hesitant to go.

However, I hated the loneliness that consumed me. How much I longed for someone to talk to and confide in. She called me as I was still debating with myself. I felt like a bird trapped in a cage, taking deep breaths on the verge of breaking free. It meant so much that someone recognized me as human. I saw in her gaze that she too experienced similar emotions and had much she desired to say.

As I thought, she wanted to know all the details shortly after I arrived. With sincerity, I shared everything. However, recalling the neighborhood kids and their mockery when they discovered my story, I imagined Suad revealing my secrets and incurring more ridicule. Changing the subject, I asked about her kidnapped husband.

"So far, I know nothing about him," she said. "I informed the authorities to search for him. A person without family or relatives has no support; it's like a branch cut off from a tree. Just like you, there is no one from my family standing by my side."

"How?" I asked.

"Many people don't have a choice. We are forced to do everything in our society, even with our affection. My sister and I were at home. She was engaged to my cousin, and I was engaged to Fahd, who is now my husband.

"After my sister passed away, my family insisted that I break up with Fahd, and marry my cousin, who used to be my sister's fiancé because tradition dictates that a cousin marries his paternal female cousin. I would never leave Fahd since our relationship was strong. We agreed and ran away together. That's why my family and cousins abandoned me and they're still angry with me.

We came to this town, which is a mixture of all the neighboring villages—where no one interferes in anyone else's affairs. I haven't seen any of my relatives for 10 years.

"Oh, Farah. No house is without worries and problems, but they remain secrets to their owners. You ask me: 'How long have you been in this house? I don't know anything about you before now.' Sometimes one fears revealing their secret for fear of other people's tongues and the gossip they spread; so, if it's suppressed, it remains like hidden thorns within them. Even I didn't tell anyone about my secrets."

"Neither you nor me are afraid of anyone because we are behaving correctly," I said. "I question how some men act as they please; no restrictions bind them and nobody reproaches them."

As we talked, time passed quickly.

"You need to rest," I said. "You've been tired since morning. I'll say goodbye for now; I'm going back to my house to try to sleep. I'm still worried about who left that note on the door."

Thankfully, my night was very peaceful and I slept late into the morning. When I awoke, I wished I could find someone to keep me company every day and listen to my inner thoughts and daily struggles. I was tired of talking to the papers I used to write down whatever happened. For a change, I even started looking for clothes I hadn't worn among the bundles folded in my closet. I used to wash the same clothes and wear them again. I am sure the neighbors recognized me from afar by their colors.

I went out for a falafel sandwich since I didn't have to work that day. I had an opportunity for downtime. I passed Um Adham's house, the friend of Um Sadiq. Perhaps she needed me to work. There was no other way to know but ask.

Um Adham missed me, she said. I found out from her that Um Sadiq had left her husband for good. Bu Sadiq, after his crimes were exposed, was arrested.

"You, Farah, came at the right time," Um Adham said. "Tomorrow is the neighborhood women's gathering at my house. I may need you in the morning."

"I will be back tomorrow morning, inshallah."

I walked home quickly, thinking about who had stuck the note on the door and when they might return. Another note on the door said: "I'll pass by in two days."

Who was messing with my nerves and acting like this? No one knew where I lived except for Mulham. What did he want from me? Before entering the house,

I knocked on my neighbor Suad's door to check on her and any news about her husband. Her son told me that she went to the market to sell her jewelry because the kidnapper demanded ransom. The criminal had already stolen his father's savings.

I tore the note off the door and angrily closed it behind me. Silence awaited me in my room. Everything stared at me. What was missing was a radio. How eagerly I wanted to hear Um Kulthum's singing. Her voice comforted my soul.

The next day, I woke early and went to Um Adham's house, wondering what awaited me. I had not felt comfortable with her in Um Sadiq's house because she interfered with everyone's life. I told myself, I will endure her for today.

***

CHAPTER 5

Twenty bundles of parsley were waiting for me, and Um Adham instructed me to make the chopping consistent, refusing to accept any piece larger than another. She told me that once when a friend invited the ladies' group to a feast, the parsley was delicious but chopped unevenly. Her guests ate the entire tabbouleh. After they left, though, they gossiped about her food and criticized her. She said she didn't accept people gossiping behind her back.

"That's people's nature," I said. "They overlook positive things and only talk about the negatives. The saying goes: 'If you light up your ten fingers as candles for some people, they still won't be grateful.'"

She went to tend to her children's requests, and returned speaking about chopping parsley.

"This cut is small, this one is large."

I swallowed my irritation and reworked it, trying to please her.

Still, I had trouble tolerating her comments, and the noise she made clattering dishes gave me a headache. I still had to prepare kibbeh, which takes a long time. I expected Um Adham to help me, but even though she was over 60, she couldn't fry an egg. It became clear she always ordered fast food from restaurants.

After finishing everything, I had to tidy the kitchen. I could hear the voices of the guests and everything they talked about. Um Adham's distinctive voice rang, "I got the kibbeh and tabbouleh from the finest restaurants!"

After everyone told her how delicious the food was they asked which restaurant. She became flustered. Her mouth went dry and she stumbled over her words.

"My husband brought everything—I don't know from where," she said.

I was astonished by her lies. Her deception struck me like lightning—I had prepared everything and credit for my hard work went straight to the restaurant. I couldn't focus on arranging the kitchen utensils anymore. Distracted and upset, a plate slipped from my hands and shattered on the floor.

Um Adham heard the noise and entered, anger on her face.

"May God break your hand," she said loudly. "What have you done? I'll deal with you later!"

I secretly thought, "If the plate were still in my hands, I would hit your face!"

It crossed my mind to leave. But I needed the payment. I'd earned it, enduring her scolding while fulfilling demands.

In the living room, an interesting conversation was taking place among them. I wished to sit, join their conversation, and put forth my point of view. Together, they had established a fund to help high-achieving students who needed financial support complete their education. But they saw me as ignorant, knowing nothing about life other than washing dishes and cleaning houses.

I'd endure everything until the day's end, and this woman wouldn't see my face again, even if I died starving. My legs could no longer carry me due to exhaustion and hunger. It had been so hard to bear hunger while having food in my hands. However, my pride didn't allow me to taste the food in this despicable woman's house.

Um Adham came and asked me to leave, as she no longer needed me. I prepared myself hesitantly, as she hadn't given me wages for the work. She glared irritably and said, "Get out!"

"But you haven't paid me yet?" I said

"Pay for what? Did you forget you broke a plate?"

"One plate? Compared to a full day's work?"

"Don't you know that now the whole dozen plates are ruined? How am I supposed to serve this set of plates to my guests with one missing?"

I didn't answer because it's pointless to argue with someone like her. She might create trouble I didn't need. There's no doubt she had no conscience. I left the house and saw her daughter, Duha, putting her two pampered dogs in the car. I hoped Duha would offer me a ride since I struggled to walk with worn-out legs and worn-out shoes. As I continued walking, my feet slipped from the shoes and I decided to walk barefoot. Suddenly, a car stopped next to me and the driver called out, offering me a ride. I thanked him but declined since I didn't know him. However, he quickly got out of the car, took off his slippers, and asked me to wear them before he went on his way. After he left his slippers on the sidewalk and drove off, I put them on and continued with a growling stomach.

Upon arriving home, I went straight to the kitchen for something to eat. I heard light knocks on the front door. It was my neighbor Suad waiting for my return with a feast in celebration of her husband's release. He'd been freed for a ransom of 25 million pounds (approximately $20,000 (U.S.) at the time). I congratulated Suad on her husband's safe return from the criminals who had spread chaos and pain throughout their country.

I enjoyed a traditional mansaf dish, fried kibbeh, and bulgur. Soon after, I was overcome with drowsiness. In my room, I fell asleep but my subconscious stayed awake. Nightmares troubled me. How did this tiring day of work for Um Adham pass without reward?

I recalled the conversations among the ladies gathered. They discussed the plight of young girls. They sought solutions for youth leaving the country and the increasing number of unmarried women, but didn't feel like they'd achieved much success on those national issues. However, they were allocating a specific amount throughout the academic career of several deserving girls right here.

***

CHAPTER 6

I often spent my time browsing through what happened to me in people's homes and forgetting my own loneliness and isolation, so that hope remained when I worked in a new house. That day, I resolved not to leave the house, perhaps able to find out who posted the note on the door. Knowing it was almost certainly Mulham, I was eager to see him.

Still, I was worried about getting to know each other more and his discovery that I'd denied him vital details of my life—a life that no one had accepted thus far. Was it reasonable for this society not to accept me as a human being, and never understand the woman who gave birth to me? Even if I found plenty of reasons for her actions, I refused to forgive her for the position she had put me in.

In my childhood, I used to hear Um Bassam talking to friends. She alone could justify what my biological mother had done.

"As long as we do not know the truth about that woman, we cannot blame anyone," she'd say. "What is this child's crime? A popular proverb says: 'The one who raises the child is the parent, not the one who gives birth!'"

Some days passed quickly, one after another, and I'd feel powerless. My pen's ink dried from excessive scribbling. I wished to embrace a child who'd also lost its mother. There were many orphans who needed someone to hold them. My imagination wandered through the horizon, in the clouds, and across the sky, listening to the rustling of trees in the forests and watching yellow leaves fall to the ground in autumn. Then, buds would grow anew, bloom, and become green again while golden sunrays brightened everything around me.

I moved gleefully in my mind from one place to another. I awoke from my reverie after realizing my shoes in the dream were hurting my feet.

Finally, Mulham arrived, calling me from afar with a loud voice.

"Where are you, Farah? I know what happened at Um Sadiq's house and figured you'd need a job."

Without family or loved ones, it felt like he was close to me. I was eagerly seeking someone who cared and asked about me.

"Hello, Mulham," I said. "You came just in time. I am jobless and in need of many things."

"I came to tell you that my aunt, Um Saleh, is ill and needs someone to take care of her. Please come with me so I can introduce you to her."

"Wait for me a little bit. I will get ready."

I emerged wearing the slippers the car driver left me. Mulham looked at me.

"Are you going like this?" he asked.

Feeling uncertain, I didn't answer.

"Wait until I return," he said.

He hurriedly left and returned with the shoes he bought for me.

"I hope they fit!" I said.

"Indeed, I hope so," he said. "Let's head to Um Saleh's house."

I thanked him and insisted he accept my reimbursement after I'd received my first earnings from Um Saleh. Mulham's excessive care aroused my suspicion.

***

CHAPTER 7

I was in for a big surprise at the house of Mulham's Auntie. It was Um Saleh, who I already knew. The old woman looked like an angel on her bed, with light emanating from her face, and cleanliness in every corner of the house, even though she couldn't sit up on her own. Her elderly friend sat beside her, and they were chatting. After greeting Um Saleh, I entered the kitchen to see if it needed organizing or cleaning, but there was no work for me there.

I returned to Um Saleh and asked what I could do. She replied in a gentle voice, "Stay by my side as I might need help. Sit down, my daughter."

She continued her conversation with her friend Um Ammar.

"May God protect my son's wife," Um Saleh said. "She wakes up early, cleans and tidies my house, prepares my breakfast, gives me medication, prepares lunch, caters to her husband's and children's needs, and then goes to work."

"May God bless her," Um Ammar said. "Everyone in the neighborhood envies you for your son's wife and her kindness."

"Do you know where our old neighbor Um Amer is?" Um Saleh asked. "I haven't seen anyone from her family lately. Where is she?"

"Um Amer was taken to a home for the elderly," Um Ammar answered.

"Oh dear! Poor Um Amer," said Um Saleh. "She gave birth and raised her children, and she worked hard throughout her life. In her last days, no one can bear nor take care of her."

"Sister, not all people are the same," said Um Ammar. "No one can accept her situation. It's a shame. She was diagnosed with Alzheimer's, and no one knew how to deal with her. Neither her children nor their wives. Their voices would rise every day and reach the end of the alley. All her sons' wives decided to go back to their parents' houses, threatening their husbands that they wouldn't return unless they took Um Amer to a nursing home. And I'm still sitting here and I can't visit her."

I hesitated to interrupt the conversation but finally said, "What would you like me to get for you?"

With a smile on her face, Um Saleh said, "My dear, please do us a favor and make us some chamomile tea."

Um Ammar drank her cup and bid farewell to Um Saleh. Then she turned to me.

"When you finish your work here, I'll be waiting for you," Um Ammar said. "I need your help with an important matter. Our house is next to Um Saleh's house."

How I wished to stay in this home as it brought comfort to everyone who entered and gave off positive energy. Um Saleh's family showed each other kindness. One of the most beautiful moments was when her grandchildren returned from school and rushed to hug and kiss her. She embraced them with affection and love, while everyone eagerly served her.

I also saw how she spoke on the phone with her children overseas, urging them to return.

"Come back to our country," she said. "No place can accommodate you like your homeland. Otherwise, you will live as strangers abroad; even if you return after a long time, you will live as strangers in your own country."

"Mother," they'd respond. "We only realized the value and blessings of our country after being apart from it. There is nothing like our homeland—its sunshine, air, and people; but you know the circumstances. We miss you dearly and we'll bring you here to visit us."

Tears streamed down her cheeks.

"I'm afraid I might die without seeing you again!" she said.

She told me about her children and the death of their father when they were young. She explained how she took on the responsibility of raising them while working as a seamstress with a manual sewing machine.

"Thankfully, I never had to ask anyone for help until they completed their education. Now, one of them is a doctor, another an engineer, and others pursued higher studies. I had wished to die after losing two of my six boys. But my consolation is that they perished as martyrs in the war. I still have four young men—two living abroad and two still here."

She paused.

"I pray you never experience loss or being away from your loved ones, my dear."

I listened in silence, sorrowful for her suffering. I tried to choke back my emotion, but tears fell involuntarily.

"May God grant you patience," I said.

"There are many things also harder than death and missing, Auntie."

"I must have unintentionally awakened your sorrows," she said. "I know there are harder things, my dear."

"The hardest thing, Auntie, is when a person, like a fruit falling from a tree, rolls far away from the tree that bore it, and everyone sees it as a rotten fruit."

"What are you saying, my child? That's a big statement for your age. You're still young. What are you going through that's causing you pain?"

"Age is not important—whether young or old. What matters is what gets planted in our childhood and the fact that it's almost impossible to erase."

"All right, my dear. Can I know what's hurting you so I can help? Consider me your second mother. Share with me what's inside so you can feel relieved."

"When the time is right, I'll tell you everything. Now is not the right time. And it's time for me to go because Aunt Um Ammar is waiting for me."

"I will tell you something important," she said.

It was my first time at Um Saleh's house, and I wondered what she had to tell me. Before leaving, I asked, "Do you know what Um Ammar wants from me?"

"I don't know. But she's a woman who loves doing good deeds; maybe she needs something from you."

***

CHAPTER 8

I hesitantly entered Um Ammar's house. To my surprise, she turned out to be Mulham's mother. She immediately began telling me how Mulham had been in a relationship with a woman for five years. Their love story became well known throughout town, and he was waiting for the right opportunity to marry her. However, their marriage didn't happen after a terrorist tortured and raped her. She managed to escape and return to her family's house. Yet Mulham ended the relationship. He began searching for a new bride.

Um Ammar went on to say that Mulham sent his mother to Um Saleh's house, knowing I would be there. He told her about his admiration for me and expressed his desire to get closer if I wasn't committed to anyone else. I listened but could hardly bear what she said. How could he fault that woman who loved him so much and suffered so greatly?

"How is that girl doing?" I asked. "Does she still love Mulham?"

"She still loves him and writes to him, asking if they can marry, but he refuses."

How does he reject her so easily, abandoning a five-year love? She experienced this tragedy against her will. How was she unable to justify herself for him?

"My daughter, I won't deny it," Um Ammar said. "I asked the girl, in the presence of her mother, to undergo surgery to restore her virginity without her fiancé Mulham knowing about it. However, the girl replied, 'I can't lie to him and deny what happened. I don't want my life with him to begin with a lie! If he or anyone else doesn't appreciate my circumstances and what I've been through, I'd rather continue my life alone and be honest with myself.'"

"What do you think, Farah? Would you like to get closer to Mulham?"

His stance toward his ex-love left me dubious. Still, I didn't answer her negatively or positively.

"Time has a way of resolving complicated matters," I said.

I left her house and headed home for some rest and solitary time to continue documenting thoughts I hesitated to share with anyone. I was surprised by the way Um Ammar talked about her son. I suppose I noticed his interest to some extent, but why couldn't Mulham express his admiration for me without his mother's intervention? Are failed marriages and the spread of divorce making people return to traditional marriage habits through relatives? Why couldn't Mulham have the courage to talk to me about this?

I disregarded the idea of being with him, because I was sure if I revealed my story, he would not accept me. I needed genuine love from someone who stood by me, and protected me from vulnerabilities that each woman faces.

These days, social media has invaded everyone's houses, too. It interferes with numerous values, customs, traditions, warmth, love, and kindness that once brought people together; its misuse has led to the fragmentation of families. We witness them during holidays as family members' minds are scattered here and there in a virtual life far from the home atmosphere. And while social media invades the community inside the home the war invades the community outside.

I used to live in a cozy world in Um Bassam's house, where she always gathered family members and shared life lessons, preserving the values on which they were raised. She emphasized honesty when dealing with others as well as with oneself. Down the road, as I continued to work in Um Saleh's house, I would again find this sincerity. They connected through conversation, love, and a shared dining table. In my line of work, I had entered many homes, and it became clear that only a scarce few of the successful families lived in genuine love. For the rest, the woman stood by her husband for the sake of the children, unable to sacrifice shelter or an extended family without being financially independent.

I had to continue searching for Bu Fares, the chicken seller, and ask the whereabouts of his daughter Fidda. Perhaps she was my mother, as Um Bassam said. She wasn't sure, though, as she'd only heard from neighbors. I wanted to talk to Um Saleh, who was also old enough to have gleaned information from around town. I got dressed and headed to her house.

On the way, though, I realized I still had time. I noticed nature and its beauty. It looked like the sun at its first rise, with a cool breeze with the onset of summer. I walked leisurely, enjoying nature's details. I saw birds flitting through branches and landing among various flowers. I listened to sounds coming from here and there. I observed farmers returning from their vineyards with smiles on their faces, carrying grapes and figs on their animals. They were so generous to offer some to everyone who passed.

I reached Um Saleh's house with grapes and figs in hand.

"Where did you get these fruits?" she said. After telling her about the generous vineyard farmers whom I'd seen on the way, I relied on the old saying, "God gives you to give to others."

We sat and ate fruits while she asked what Um Ammar wanted.

"She asked me if I was seeing anyone and told me that Mulham was attracted to me."

I waited for Um Saleh to say anything about Mulham or give her opinion. She didn't say anything, good or bad. She just changed the subject

"What food are you preparing for us today?" she asked.

"You can choose whatever you want, Um Saleh," I said.

"It's been a long time since you cooked chicken for us. How about having that delicious chicken dish?"

I decided now was the time to ask about Bu Faris, the chicken seller. We talked first about how he used to go around the village and neighboring villages selling live chickens. We'd buy the chickens alive, before slaughtering and cleaning them at home. As technology advanced, though, we started buying chickens already slaughtered, cleaned, and ready to cook—sometimes even grilled.

"Oh, what days those were!" Um Saleh said. "Even though they were tiring, there was a certain charm to them. It was so peaceful back then, Farah; everything was natural during our time."

"By the way, Um Saleh, where is Bu Faris now? What is he doing? Is he still selling chickens?"

"Oh Farah, it has been a long time since I last saw him. He used to come visit his daughter Fadia. Fadia lived in this town, close to our house. But then there was the scandal with his other daughter, Fidda, who ran away to her sister Fadia's house, because her father threatened to kill her."

"What did she do for him to threaten her like that?"

"I don't know exactly. People said that she had an illegitimate child and left it at the mosque's door. They also said that a woman from town found the baby and took her in—raising her alongside her own kids. This was about twenty years ago; I haven't seen Bu Faris since. What made you remember him?"

"I remembered him calling out, 'Chicken... Chiiiiiicken' in a loud voice since I was a child—how I used to call my mom to buy us one for lunch. Poor Fidda. Is she still alive or did her dad kill her?"

"She still lives on," Um Saleh said. "Her sister, Fadia, arranged her marriage to her husband's brother, who had traveled to Dubai. He fled to avoid military service and never returned to the country. Fidda joined him and lived with him in comfort, giving birth to a daughter. However, poor Fidda, I was told that her husband tragically died in a car accident in Dubai. As for Fidda and her daughter, they remain abroad, but I heard from her sister Fadia that they plan to return to the country someday."

"Um Saleh, there's no time to continue our conversation. I must start preparing the food, as the children are coming home from school hungry soon."

"Don't be late in the kitchen, Farah. I'll be waiting for you."

I headed to the kitchen with a new thread sewn into my story. It seemed that people were right about Fidda and she must be my mother. The news stirred old emotions and increased my hope of seeing her. Could I really forgive her for abandoning me, though?

As the food cooked, conflicting thoughts carried me away. What would Um Saleh's reaction be if she knew the truth about me being Fidda's daughter? No doubt she is different from others. She's wise in her thinking.

Um Saleh called for me. I hurried, asking if she wanted lunch prepared now.

"No, let's wait for the rest of the family to have lunch together," she said.

"Everything is ready, dear Um Saleh," I said. "I'm leaving now."

"I will not accept your leaving without eating lunch first. Then, you may go. But now I won't let you leave, Farah."

"I promise to eat with you another time but I must go now."

"It is not acceptable that you leave without eating or—"

"I can't eat from the food before you all do."

"No, my dear Farah. You're like my own daughter or even closer because she's far away. You are closer to me than my daughter. Go then and prepare your food while we talk until the work is done."

I entered the kitchen, pondering how people can act and think so differently. I prepared a plate of food and sat beside Um Saleh as she started asking about my life. I had to tell her: I was the girl that Um Bassam found at the mosque door.

"I never forgot, Um Saleh, my auntie, who defended me to protect my feelings," I said, "justifying the sin of those who bore me, and not letting anyone speak ill of me. Unfortunately, I was the only survivor when the bombs fell on our house. Until now, I have not told anyone about my story except you. You are the only one my conscience is comfortable with, and I can't bear it inside anymore; I haven't found anyone who understands me as you do."

My eyes were watching Um Saleh, fearing her reaction and a different way of looking at me. However, as I expected, she remained calm. All she did was reply to me with a deep sigh that alleviated my worry.

"My daughter Farah, there are others like you," she said. "You must always be stronger than the disaster to continue your life, and God willing, the coming days will be more beautiful. When I travel to Dubai, I promise to try to find your mother through one of her friends and tell her about you in my own way."

My heartbeats quickened, and my hope for life grew—hoping that one day I would meet my mother, even if it took a long time. After a silence, she asked me about Mulham.

"I don't know anything about Mulham. To tell you the truth, Um Saleh, sometimes I feel empty of emotions towards men. It's a strange feeling that keeps me from living like other girls. I have many questions inside but also sometimes feel that I need someone to live with. Despite this, my thoughts seem contradictory and impossible to control. Would you allow me to leave now, Um Saleh?"

"I miss you so much, Farah, as you don't visit us during the summer holidays. My son's wife says she takes on the responsibility of working at home during all those days off. Please accept this gift from me, and I hope you visit us during the summer holidays."

"Thank you so much, Dear Um Saleh. Inshallah, I will visit you."

I needed to be gracious, but I was confused and angry after learning I wouldn't be able to work there for the summer after all. I wondered where I'd find work. I left Um Saleh's house hardly able to see straight and collided with a wall. Suddenly, Mulham was standing at his door nearby, smiling as if he had been waiting to speak with me. He invited me into his house, saying that his mother was waiting for me. I thanked him and hurried on my way under the scorching afternoon sun. To my surprise, he drove by in his car and offered me a ride I accepted.

"Why do you look so angry?" he asked as we drove. "Have I done something to upset you?"

"You have nothing to do with my anger. I'm mad at Um Saleh because there's no work available in her house during the summer vacation; I was comfortable dealing with her and I don't like meeting new people daily whom I know nothing about. I wish I could work as a maid in just one household instead of entering an unfamiliar house every day."

"Starting today, I'll take responsibility for finding your work solutions," Mulham said. "Have you thought about the issue my mother discussed with you?"

"I still need time and can't make a decision. I'm confused about it. It requires careful consideration."

"I eagerly await your decision. As for work, are you willing to take the necessary expenses and rest at home?"

"Thank you, Mulham. Work fills my time and comforts me. I won't give it up."

"I will find a job that suits you," Mulham said.

After saying goodbye, I entered the house to remove my clothes, filled with the scent of cooking and detergents I'd grown accustomed to. However, today, the cologne that Mulham wore penetrated deep within me and invigorated me. I hadn't felt this way before. Yet, I still couldn't admit to myself that I carried the emotions like any other girl.

I appreciated his attention because I needed someone by my side, but at the same time was suspicious of him. Everything left an impression. His eyes often staring, while his smooth tongue boasted about how girls loved him but he wouldn't trust them.

He continually expressed admiration for me alone, yet I didn't believe him. Sometimes I considered him someone who expressed fake emotions to women to entrap them in swirling feelings. It's possible my mother was someone who believed those kinds of words of love and was tarnished—leaving a stain on her, her family, and her child while the father faced no punishment or blame. Such is a male-dominated society that replicates sons after their fathers in their love for control, dominance, and possession of everything. They even regard women as commodities that can be taken advantage of whenever they want before discarding them and denying their rights.

Many painful things built inside me while I filled the blank pages with thoughts. I felt a tightness in my chest. All I could do now was visit my neighbor Suad. It had been a while since I last saw her and was eager to find out how she was doing.

***

CHAPTER 9

S uad sat in her home with a large amount of yarn surrounding her. She waited for someone to visit so she could share her feelings, and perhaps feel some relief. Without waiting for me to ask, she began telling me her story.

"Do you know what happened to me?" she said. "After spending all my savings and my husband's earnings from abroad as ransom for the thugs who kidnapped him, we didn't even have money left for bread. My husband borrowed money from a friend to buy a flight abroad again, while I searched for work to feed our children until he found employment. I'd met a wool vendor so I borrowed wool to knit products and pay back my debts with the proceeds.

"During one visit, he presented me with a pure gold necklace as a gift, showering me with sweet words and flirtatious comments without respecting his own age. I refused this gift and asked him to keep our relationship strictly professional. My rejection angered him, and he replied that he would only give me the wool if I signed an invoice with my full name. Since I couldn't read or write, he suggested that I put my fingerprints on it instead.

"After taking some wool worth 10,000 lira, I provided my fingerprints on the invoice and began working day and night to pay back the amount. After some time had passed, I went back to him and handed over the 10,000 lira with gratitude. To my surprise, he said, 'What are you giving me? 10,000? The amount you received for the wool you signed for was actually 100,000.'

"100,000?" I said. "How? I took less than six pounds of wool!"

"Debts from before," he said. "I'll give you just one month; if you don't pay the amount, there'll be trouble."

"I didn't argue or discuss the matter with him. It seems like he's taking revenge on me. I don't know what to do to pay. Only five days of the month remain, and I need six months. What should I do, Farah?"

"I will go to Um Saleh. This woman always loves doing good deeds, and I'll get you the money. Once you have it, you can pay it back to her."

"You're doing me a huge favor, Farah! I won't forget it."

I went to Um Saleh, and she immediately accepted my request without knowing who it was for or what I would do with it.

Suad's problem was resolved with the old man who took advantage of her. Yet I was still waiting for my situation to improve with a new job. I looked out the window, hoping Mulham would come to tell me about a new job that could make my life more secure again.

Finally too bored from sitting at home, I left not knowing where to go. Thinking about Um Saleh's new revelations about my mother and aunt, I went to Fadia's house on the pretext of asking if she needed someone to work in her home. I could learn more about my mother. I arrived at the home described by Um Saleh. Hesitantly, I climbed the stairs wondering how she would receive me. After ringing the doorbell, a woman welcomed me.

"Is this Fadia's house?" I asked.

"I am Fadia. Who are you, and what do you want from me?"

"I was told that you need someone to work in your house?"

"What is your name, and where did you used to work?"

"I am Farah, and I used to work at your neighbor's house, Um Saleh. Ask Um Saleh about me if you'd like!"

She asked for my phone number, which I gave her.

"If I need you, I will call you."

I started back to my house with high hopes. Maybe I was a step closer to learning something about my mother or even meeting her. It was late afternoon and still very hot. I decided to stop at the park. I sat on a bench next to a happy young couple and enjoyed sunflower seeds I'd bought from a poor man selling them at the park's front gate.

I looked at the other park-goers, hoping to see some women I might know. I didn't. The woman sitting on the bench caught my attention, though. They seemed extremely happy, their eyes sparkling as they exchanged loving glances and whispers. It sounded as if they were talking about their wedding. However, within a second, their expressions changed, and anger ruled their faces. Suddenly, the girl raised her voice, insulting the young man and criticizing him. She removed her engagement ring and threw it at him. The ring missed him but hit me under my eye.

While the woman quickly left the park, the young man started searching for the ring. After picking it off the ground he hurried after her. Meanwhile, I was bewildered and bloodied. I found a tissue to soak the blood. I pressed against the wound, which caught the attention of those around me. They rushed over, wanting to help. One woman convinced me to go to the nearest health center while another accompanied me. She told me it was strange that I had no company at the park.

I told her I was alone in this village. While looking down so my eyes would avoid betraying my lie, I said my family were victims of the war. With a deep sigh, she apologized.

"The war has caused many wounds that we cannot forget," she said.

We reached the health center. They questioned me.

"Who hurt you and caused this wound? Who were you fighting with? Where is your ID card?"

They seemed to forget about all the kidnapping, killing, and smuggling crimes happening around us. Instead, they scrutinized a small accidental wound. I felt flustered. However, the woman accompanying me saved more trouble. She convinced the doctor my story was true and he nursed the wound and bandaged it.

We left the center, and I thanked the woman who treated me kindly without knowing who I was.

At sunset, I was apprehensive on my way back home. So many people now carry weapons without hesitating to use them. I entered the alley quickly, my heart pounding. Before getting inside, Suad called to me, inviting me for yerba mate. A delicious smell of food wafted from her house. I assumed she had a large pot cooking and guests. The women in our alley knew her food was exceptional.

"I'll come back another time," I said.

She insisted I come have tea, though.

"Do you have guests?"

"No, Farah, there's no one here but I am cooking. One day the neighbors had an event at their house and all the invited guests loved the food I prepared. They asked, 'Who made the food?' Then, other women started asking me whether I could cook for their events. You know the situation, Farah, and the debts I have, and how long it would take me to pay them off. So, I agreed to work from my home for my neighbor and her acquaintances."

I was happy she'd found a job. She soon asked about my eye, and I told her the story, including the questionable treatment at the health center.

That night, I slept heavily and dreamed of Fadia saying she needed me to work. I was surprised upon entering her home, seeing a woman with her seventeen-year-old daughter. It was my mother Fidda, who had come on a trip with her daughter. I went immediately to the kitchen, and Fadia instructed me that her sister, Fidda, craved traditional foods. She told me I needed to prepare it well.

"What would you like to eat, Fidda?" my aunt asked her sister.

"I'm craving kibbeh bil laban," my mother said.

I was trying to make the food better than ever before. Their high-pitched voices expressed joy in reuniting. I heard my Aunt Fadia talking to Fidda's beautiful daughter.

"Oh Eileen, how much you resemble your mother. Look at her carefully."

"There is no problem," Eileen said. "She is a respected person. But certainly, circumstances forced her to work in houses. You are judging her. If only you knew how to prepare this dish like her."

I ran toward Eileen and kissed her. She hugged me back. How much I wished that I could have kissed my mother before waking up. I tossed and turned in my bed until the next day. I wanted my dreams to become reality.

That day, my neighbor, Suad, asked me to go with her mother-in-law to the hospital. Suad said she couldn't go with her, not wanting to leave the children home alone and that her mother-in-law might have to stay in the hospital for tests.

***

CHAPTER 10

There were painful scenes in the hospital. I sat next to Um Sultan, glancing left and right. Some patients were near the end of their lives. Some were just beginning their battle with illnesses at a young age. Patients with wandering eyes glanced at other patients' beds, with looks full of fear, terror, and sadness. I watched them, feeling pain from the suffering and misery in their eyes.

I told myself that if I were wealthy I would allocate a private place for each person. Then, they wouldn't have to see others suffering. I did see some new patients smiling when they entered for the first time. Then, the shock was too powerful.

Many questions came to mind: How much money was wasted on killing people? How many houses were destroyed? How much money was stolen while thousands desperately needed care and medication?

I looked around, swatting flies from Um Sultan's face. Although we could keep flies out of our homes, they swarmed in hospitals. An old woman lying on a bed opposite Um Sultan caught my attention. Flies landed on her face as she took what could be her final breaths. Nobody was beside her. I put a chair between the two beds and chased the hovering flies from both their faces.

Some health supervisors checked on that woman before her son finally arrived with a bag of medicine, anxious to check on her. He bent and embraced her, kissing her hands, head, and even feet, apologizing for not being able to come sooner. Upon hearing his voice, she opened her eyes and tears poured. She tried to speak but couldn't. Instead, she shook her head as if blaming him: You're just now coming, my son? Then she tried once more to say something. His name was her last word. And then a farewell glance. The tragedy was that her son was working in a foreign country. He couldn't come to see her until her last moments.

Meanwhile, Um Sultan's health kept worsening. Suad spent her time between the hospital and home, where she needed to care for the children and cook for neighbors to make money. She called her husband about his mother's illness, insisting he return and stays by her side during her last days. I heard Suad's side of the conversation and she later reported on what her husband said. He told her he hadn't found a job yet, as it had only been a month since he'd left. He asked Suad to keep him updated on his mother's condition so he could return if needed.

"Tell me, Suad," he finally asked. "Who is staying in the hospital to take care of her?"

"Our neighbor Farah is with her day and night," Suad said.

Suad left the hospital to attend to their children, and I was growing tired of sitting on a chair day and night. There was no bed for me. At times I found solace in talking to the patients' relatives who were also care-givers. Most were women who tried engaging their loved ones in conversation to try distracting them from the pain.

One woman sat at the edge of a bed where her sick daughter's fever spiked. The mother dampened a towel with cold water and dabbed the girl's feet and forehead while praying for her recovery. Eventually, they both fell asleep.

Across from them sat another woman while her daughter slept deeply after taking painkillers. Around midnight, the mother had become severely drowsy after staying awake so long. She fell, and I failed in trying to catch her. The mother on the edge of the bed awoke. I helped the woman who fell get up before leaving to get Um Sultan water. I returned to hear the two women in conversation. They were once neighbors and recalled memories.

"How long ago did you travel abroad, Um Issam?" asked one.

"A long time ago, when people were living simply. They would sleep in their courtyards or on rooftops because of the heat without fear of others. Oh, Um Ghayth, upon my return to this country, everything had changed in people's behavior; their doors only opened on special occasions. Do you remember when we used to sleep together on the rooftop of your provisions house?"

"I remember everything that has passed, may God bless us. Neighbors didn't differentiate between their house and their neighbor's house. I recall that summer moonlit night when an unexpected guest who missed the last bus to the city surprised us, calling out loudly: 'Hello people of this house!' Everyone woke up and prepared food for him in the middle of the night in case he was hungry. After getting acquainted, he spent the rest of the evening with us under moonlight.

"I traveled in those days, when people's gatherings were intimate and they spoke sincerely and lovingly with each other. Not like now when people talk more to virtual people than real ones. Those lovely days I miss. I felt like a stranger abroad and now I feel the same in my homeland after the bonds of affection and communication have been severed between people. I remember when someone would call out for help, and everyone in the town would rush to their aid, whether it was a fire, a flood, or something about their livestock. When I left a long time ago, all our neighbors came to bid us farewell, but we didn't see any of them upon our return; oh, how beautiful the past was, Um Ghayth. The students respected their teacher; the child respected their parents.

"Nowadays there's nothing but rebellion against everything meaningful; even young girls who lived in innocence and respect have now been corrupted by a distorted society. Those days when we could wander the streets without fear whether it was day or night. Today, as soon as the sun sets, it's as if there's a curfew in place. God bless those days when we shared bread, salt, and water with one another. Now I see none of this; it's like social bonds between people have deteriorated. And corruption, kidnappings, and killings spread as if they're ordinary or meaningless matters.

"Have you seen the situation we've come to, Um Issam?" Um Ghayth said. "Even the diseases spread, sicknesses we've never heard of before."

"I know, Um Ghayth. The reason is the greedy people who care only about money. Their last concern is humanity, which has become a victim of the chemicals and manipulation within our food. That's why these diseases exist."

I had never heard anything like it before, unaware of what they were talking about. I knew about gunfire, explosions, and smoke rising. Meanwhile, we all were consuming toxic substances in our food, with countless victims suffering. After a period of silence, I heard their deep sighs. They each placed their hands on their cheeks.

Um Issam stared at Um Ghayth and asked, "Did you doze off?"

Um Ghayth didn't respond. Um Issam glanced around the room to check who was awake, eager to continue talking. She adjusted her seat and leaned on the edge of the bed beside her feverish daughter. I dozed for a moment and woke when the nurse called, "Farah, get the patient ready! We're taking her to the X-ray room!" Despite all that's happening in the country, hospitals still offer vital services to patients.

In the morning, I saw a young woman caring for an elderly patient by offering her a cup of milk. Once the patient took the cup, she couldn't balance it with her trembling hand. The milk spilled on her clothes and floor. The woman, who turned out to be her daughter-in-law, yelled at the patient.

"What's wrong with you? I have to clean up after you!"

She kept mumbling and cursing her misfortune, regretting that she'd ever met the woman's son. The patient's tears flowed, and she rested her head on the pillow as she told her daughter-in-law: "Thank you so much, darling. God willing, you'll never be sick in your life or need anyone's help."

The daughter-in-law looked around as she cleaned up the milk, thinking other patients hadn't noticed her; however, she found everyone staring at her disapprovingly because of what she had said. She tried to cover her rudeness by offering another cup of milk and speaking to the older woman quietly now. Her mother-in-law rejected it, telling her to let her sleep.

A doctor who'd examined Um Sultan came to tell me her condition was stable, with no imminent danger. Yet a blood clot had formed on her right side, and it would take some time for her to recover. He would discharge her from the hospital and prescribe medication and physical therapy at home. I couldn't wait to go home and rest after losing so much sleep during those days at the hospital.

Suad accompanied Um Sultan to her house, while I went to the supermarket. I was surprised by the loud voices and the fight in the store. Someone called the police because a customer had bought some bread but stole a can of beans. He was caught on camera. Everyone realized he only had enough money for bread. People sympathized with him, some giving him money and others buying him food. The poor man left everything behind, even the bread he paid for, muttering, "If it were a bank robbery, such a fuss wouldn't have even happened."

I thought about the poor man and how they made a big case out of stealing a can of beans—forgetting the country's problems and what war does to people like him. I asked myself: What has led us here? No one listens to another. Have people or times changed? My thoughts went unanswered.

—

Daily stress makes me hurt for others. I am constantly tense, like an official concerned about their country's affairs. No one cares about me, though. I have no family or relatives. People insult me for working in a different house every day. It's simple, though.

When I work in people's homes, I eat. When I don't work, I don't eat.

I didn't sleep before all my haunting thoughts returned: meeting my mother, trying to justify what she did, forgiving her. Maybe, I would fall asleep to happy dreams and wake up optimistic and ready for a beautiful day.

In the morning, I would meet Heba, a maid who promised to get me a job at the house where she worked. She was leaving and wanted me to take her place.

***

CHAPTER 11

Heba told me all about working at Nizar's house on our way.

"I have been working in their home for five years, and they trust me as if I were one of their family members," she said. "They are rich people, they have a lot of property, and they pay me a high wage, which no one else gives to housekeepers."

"Why are you going to leave this house, Heba?" I asked in surprise.

"I'm going to leave the country with my sister," she said.

After introducing me to Nizar's family, Heba insisted she spend a week with me to train me about everything in the house. We worked every day, but we also had fun gossiping.

"What do you do after work, Farah?" she asked.

"I rest at home," I said. "And look back on what happened that day and write in my notebook."

"I am smarter than you, Farah," she said and laughed. "After I finish my work, I like to play with the feelings of boys."

"What are you saying?" I said. "Normally, boys play with girls' feelings. Why do you do that?"

"I will not hide from you, Farah, I am a girl like other girls. I have feelings and a heart that beats with love and likes beauty. I am pretty, aren't I?" she said. "Listen to me, Farah, I will tell you about one of my adventures with boys. There's a young man who seduced me by his looks, elegance, beauty, and green eyes."

Whenever I went out with him, I took so much time making myself up that he thought I was rich. We always met in the gardens. Sometimes, we walked to the markets. I had been lying to him, and he believed I was a university student. He promised to marry me, but I didn't believe him. I just didn't tell him that.

"I used to always see him with other girls after my work was finished, and he didn't pay attention because I was in my work clothes.

"I finally got tired of that guy. He evaded everything I asked of him under flimsy pretenses. He was pretending to be what he was not. He didn't even spend a single pound on me. The last time we met, he was more than an hour late. I was waiting for him while the sun was scorching hot. When he arrived at the place where we'd always met he said he had car problems.

"I told him that I was tired from standing under the scorching sun and that we had to sit somewhere. He suggested walking, and I said: 'I cannot walk. I am tired and hungry. I want to rest, and we are near a popular restaurant.' I went toward the restaurant while he was walking behind me muttering. I entered, sat at a table, and asked for a food menu, and, as usual, he ignored me and started talking on his phone nearby without ever taking a seat. Then, while I was looking at the menu, he left.

"An elegant, attractive young man was sitting alone at a table next to me. He was trying to figure out what was going on between us. I noticed he was looking for a way to talk to me. I was surprised when he approached and invited me to sit. I agreed. I intended to play with his feelings just like the other young men. Some of them were rich and still wouldn't even buy me a falafel sandwich."

"What are these ways, Heba?" I asked. "I do not like such reckless behavior. It causes problems."

"I know, Farah, it is a bad habit. Young people always play with each other's feelings. It is a reaction and revenge for what I lived through that I cannot forget. When my father was beating my mother and abusing her, she tried to save herself and run away. I stayed with my brothers, all of us young, spending our days in the streets without food. My father neglected us, and we were begging people for a meager meal. Nobody took care of us, nor taught us in school. I am sure, Farah, that there will come a day when I will become rich and live a stable life. And there is only a short time left before I say goodbye and travel with my sister."

While spending my time with Heba at work, I didn't feel tired despite the house being very big. I hadn't liked her behavior, but I soon missed her so much when she left me alone. Our conversations had led us to so many interesting subjects.

While working in the house alone, I began wondering more: Why is this house so big? Three floors and only two people live in it! Nizar and his wife Huda. Yet so many people are sleeping in the streets and homeless because of the war. Working in it had suddenly become very tiring.

Nizar and his wife also missed Heba, who spent five years in their house eating and drinking with them at the same table. They were always talking about how she filled the house with fun and gave them energy.

She would tell them about her adventures with boys, too, and how she would play with their feelings.

So, Heba's absence created a void for everyone. I worked all day long, and I didn't find anyone else to have fun with. Although I had no time to rest in that house, I still became bored. I was thinking of looking for another house to escape my loneliness. I decided to look for a job the next morning, before I returned to work at Nizar's house.

That was the plan anyway. The next morning, someone knocked on my door. I didn't expect to see a policeman and that the police would search for me for a reason that didn't say. They arrested me on a charge of robbery and took me to the neighborhood police station. A preliminary investigation was carried out, and their questions made it clear that Nizar's wife, Huda, claimed I had stolen her jewelry.

How difficult it was to be accused of a crime you didn't commit. For me, though, it made little difference at first since I sometimes felt as if I lived in an open prison, with hard labor all day and a house that now added psychological hardship.

After they'd searched the house I was renting and didn't find anything, I was peppered with questions: Whose daughter are you? Where does your family live? I replied that my family had died in the war. They didn't believe me. They went to the town where I lived, searching for Um Bassam's house in particular. They didn't find landmarks for where it had once been nor for the population center nearby. It was all destroyed.

Every day, the investigator summoned me. "You have to confess!" he'd say. He threatened me with torture if I didn't. How could I admit to something I didn't do? It was useless to question me. I started believing it was Heba who stole the jewelry, as she was planning to leave the country.

I believed that torture wouldn't be more difficult than the life I already lived. Before I entered the torture chamber, though, a girl's scream from within tore my heart open. I saw a young man whipping her hard, before exiting quickly and saying, "In a little while I will come back for you."

I thought I'd heard this young man's voice before. Yet in my anger, I couldn't place it. I'd seen the girl before. Her name was Samar, and I introduced myself. Her beauty, even after what she'd suffered, caught my attention.

"You ought not to be hit even with a rose, Samar," I said. "Is it reasonable for everything this criminal did to you?"

"When that monster comes, oh Farah," she said. "Get ready."

I started becoming afraid and whispered, "What is your crime, Samar?"

"It is all because of these men who do not fear God," she said.

At this moment, a tall young man with broad shoulders entered with a frown. He wasn't the young man who'd whipped Samar.

"Who is Farah?" he asked.

"I am Farah."

I expected my innocence to be proven and that he'd come to tell me about my release. I hadn't stolen anything in my life. Even though I was in need. When I worked in houses, I would avoid looking at valuable things.

Yet he soon brought me into the chamber and began to whip me to the point where I didn't think I could bear any more.

Fortunately, there was a holiday the following day and we couldn't be punished. That's when Samar told me her story.

"Since I was young, I loved studying and excelled until entering the university.

I didn't care about anything except my education. The young men used to challenge each other to talk to me because of my seriousness. I didn't want to go out and deal with guys. I didn't even respond to them.

"One time, my friend Haifa, who was dear to my heart and I trusted, invited me to her house. She surprised me with a gift of pajamas, and insisted I try them on before I left her house. I changed in her bedroom. She complimented me.

"When I returned home the misfortunes began. My phone rang, but I didn't answer for an unfamiliar number. A young man then sent pictures of me on WhatsApp. They were from me in Haifa's bedroom, without any clothes on. I knew my dear friend, Haifa, was complicit with this young man, Rawad, who must have been hiding in the bedroom. They were trying to blackmail me. I remembered him well because he was very thick-headed in school. He used to never leave his friend Iyad. They had many problems with girls.

"When I didn't respond to Rawad's pictures, he started threatening me: 'If you don't do what I ask of you, I will send these pictures to your father!'

"Haifa didn't answer my call. I visited her house several times and she wasn't there. Rawad was a villain. He teamed with his friend Iyad to humiliate me more. I became the slutty bitch girl when I was actually focused on excelling in my studies. My father heard the story about me from people's whispers. To avoid problems, he married me off to an 80-year-old without my consent. It was better than committing a crime and killing me to defend our family's honor.

"Days passed, and a volcano ignited inside me to take revenge. Finally, I met Haifa, who hadn't been anywhere in sight. She came back, though, after having heard I got married. I calmed enough to convince her things had been going smoothly now. There was nothing wrong with inviting her friends, Rawad and Iyad, to her house, I said. I wanted to apologize to Rawad for getting married and denying his interest. We met in Haifa's house. I only talked about our old school days, and how poor Rawad and Iyad had done at school. My calmness did not help me enough, though, because my blood was still boiling over Haifa's role in the mess and how she might have benefitted. I only knew 'She did not maintain the bond of the bread and the salt,' I thought had been between us. She was like a snake. I considered how my future and psyche were destroyed, without getting anything from this loss.

"I took out a can of acid to take revenge. I didn't care if my end would be execution. It was better than living with that old man my father had married me off to because of them. I saw them burning. I usually am very calm and peaceful by nature, but their violence had now inspired violence in me.

"Here, I am awaiting execution, and there is no difference for me between dying or staying alive. As for you, Farah, the truth will come out and your innocence will emerge."

"The truth, Samar," I said. "It is real torture for any person who enters a prison innocent. Samar, I am innocent."

A policeman entered calling Samar. He said a visitor had asked about her. It turned out to be the husband her father married her off to. He'd come to find out what happened to her, but she refused to meet him.

"Why didn't you see him?" I asked. "Isn't it enough that he's asking about you? It's possible he could help you by hiring a lawyer to defend you."

"I didn't ask for help from anyone, and nothing concerns me in this life," she said. "Imagine, Farah, that I get out of prison one day. Would I live like everyone else? How would society treat me as a jailbird?"

"I'm quite the opposite, Samar," I said. "I hope someone will ask about me."

"You are innocent, Farah. You have the right to defend yourself or have someone from your family defend you. Farah, where is your family? So far no one has come of them."

"My story is very complicated, Samar. I will tell you about it later."

A policeman entered so we shut up. He was holding a girl's hand and cursing her.

"Where will you escape justice outside the country?" the man said.

He punched her so hard, she collapsed into the wall and fell to the ground. I was stunned to see it was Heba. I whispered to Samar.

"Inshallah, my innocence will be proven. This is Heba, who I told you about. She is the one who stole the jewelry from Nizar's house."

I looked at Heba with hatred, but she looked away as if she didn't know me. Soon, the policeman called me to receive visitors. It was Nizar and his wife Huda. She hugged me and apologized.

"How much I loved Heba, Farah, I missed her, and I trusted her very much. She was arrested at the airport trying to leave the country. The jewelry was still in her bag. Inshallah, soon they will release you. I will forgive

Heba, and I will drop my rights to punish her because I do not like to hurt anyone. I know Heba very well since she has been in my house for five years. I have never lost anything. She has the right to dream of living like everyone else. She became involved with a young man, and they agreed to leave the country together. I suspect this young man is the one who put her up to stealing."

"She is here," I said about Heba. "And thank God the truth has come to light."

"I am waiting for you when you are released and I hope that you will return to my house, Farah."

I said to myself, If I die of starvation, I will not return to you.

She noticed my expression change and asked, "Do you need anything, Farah?"

"Thank you, Mrs. Huda. I do not need anything!"

When I returned to the cell, I didn't find Samar or Heba. I thought they'd gone to the bathroom but they didn't come back. I later learned they'd been summoned for investigation. I was left alone in my cell, looking around in fear, leaning on the wall and falling asleep for a moment. I woke after nightmares disturbed me. I turned and saw no one but I couldn't close my eyes again. I didn't know what time it was, thinking it could be midnight. With all quiet, I watched the door, fearing someone would open it.

A policeman did enter soon, singing as if he were at a wedding. I wondered what he was doing in the middle of the night before seeing it was Mulham. He'd never told me he was a policeman. I remembered that voice of the man whipping Samar. It was Mulam. And now he approached me.

"What are you doing here, Farah?" he asked. "Finally, your situation is under control."

He sat next to me and started talking kindly.

"They told me that you were here, and I came to help you," he said.

"Thank you, I am innocent," I said. "I expect to be released tomorrow."

"Who told you that you are innocent? If I do not help you, you will still be here."

"It does not matter if I stay or leave."

"You must be hungry. I will bring food and then we will talk."

"I am not hungry, and do not come back here."

He went out humming before returning a little while later with food.

"I was playing with your nerves," he said. "Indeed you are innocent, and tomorrow they will release you. If you need something from me, I can do it. I am on duty."

And then he left, but I couldn't fall asleep. I tried to eat something but it stuck in my throat. The night was long, and I was waiting for the sun to rise just to leave. I felt bad for how I treated Mulham. He wanted to serve me—or maybe just pity me. Either way, I treated him with disregard. Why couldn't I change my view of the opposite sex? I still worried he was taking advantage of my situation. I often thought about my mother. How her circumstances of being taken advantage of had helped cause my trouble. I was still holding on, though. I was going to prove myself.

In the morning, my happiness bounded upon release. My innocence had been proven, and I hurried home. The owner was waiting there. He had learned I'd gone to prison for theft and wanted to throw me out. He didn't believe I was innocent, but I still begged him to wait until I found another house. He began carrying my smaller furniture and throwing it outside. Then he slammed the door with me outside, before locking it and leaving. I didn't have a contract for renting or even proof of my identity. I stood at a loss thinking about where to go, thinking it might have been better if I'd stayed in prison. While Suad had been hanging the laundry, though, she'd seen and heard what was going on.

"You will stay with me, Farah," she said. "Your situation will be settled, Inshallah!" She began carrying my bags.

"Carry what is left of the luggage and follow me," she said.

We put my bags under the stairs, and I entered the room with her.

"Where were you?" she asked. "I knocked on the door several times, but I didn't find you."

"Before I tell you," I said. "I will take a hot shower to clean the dirt and germs from prison. I am itching all over my body. Please prepare the yerba mate. I miss it from your hands. Also, it is better to drink it with talk."

In the bathroom, I finally could clean that unbearable prison filth.

"Now I will tell you what happened," I said. "I was accused of stealing the jewelry of Huda, Nizar's wife. They threw me in prison."

I told her Heba was finally arrested. It turned out the young man who prompted Heba to steal said he'd marry her if she stole enough that they could travel. They were arrested before they ever left the country.

Fortunately, I heard good news from Suad. Her husband found a job. Now, she could spend time taking care of her children and teaching them. She didn't have to cook for money anymore.

Then Suad told me that a woman she knew, Um Salim, was asking about me. Um Salim needed someone to work in her house. I started falling asleep from exhaustion.

"I cannot continue the evening with you, Suad," I said. "Tomorrow, before I go to Um Salim's house, I will look for a house to live in, and after that, I will visit Um Saleh because I miss her so much."

"I do hope you are not bored with me, Farah. I wish you would live with me. The house is big. You are like my sister."

I woke to Suad's voice asking me to get up, "It is late, Farah!"

"The night passed quickly," I said.

"It was not like so many days since I moved out of home. This was the only night I could sleep without anything to worry about. How many families had been displaced and separated because of the war, Suad? How I wish to manage to find a place to live, a job, and a house in which I can rest."

***

CHAPTER 12

Before I went to Um Saleh's house, I stood nervously outside my aunt Fadia's house, hoping my mother Fuda had returned from her travels. I climbed the stairs without hesitation, planning to ask Fadia if she needed someone to work at her house. I rang the bell and Fadia opened the door.

"I told you when I needed you, I will call you," she said. "Why did you come without me asking you?"

She slammed the door so quickly it almost broke. I went downstairs, questioning her behavior.

"She did not know me, and she behaved like this," I said. "What if she knew who I was?"

Heading to Um Saleh's house, I was sad about a day that I'd started so optimistically. I didn't find Um Saleh at home but instead, people I'd never seen before. One of them said Um Saleh had left the country with her son's family. I left Um Saleh's house angry and tense, and unable to focus because of my overwhelming hunger. Lost in thought as I crossed the road, I didn't see the oncoming car. Miraculously, I survived him crashing into me, destined to continue my torturous journey through life. I woke up from being unconscious an hour later at the hospital, uncertain who sat at my bedside. It was the driver, who'd later tell me he was terrified my injuries might be more severe. He insisted on waiting for the doctor to ask about my condition.

"All test results are good and there's nothing worrisome," the doctor said. "Only some minor scratches and bruises. She can be discharged now."

"Where are you from, and where is your home?" the driver asked.

I shortened my answer by telling him the address where he could take me. We arrived at Suad's street, and I was hoping to get out there. But he insisted he stay with me to apologize to my family for what happened. I worried about what I'd tell him to prevent him from finding me out. I finally said I wasn't from this town and was just visiting my friend.

While I was getting out of the car, I wanted to check my phone but couldn't find it. Soon, I remembered it had fallen from my hand as the car hit me. The driver insisted on giving me money toward a new one.

"This is my phone number should you need something," he said.

I went to a shop nearby and bought a notebook and pen. My old notebook was full, and I needed a new one to keep from despairing over what had happened and my bad luck.

I thought back to the woman at the hospital whose bed was next to mine. She was in a coma, but once I'd recovered enough I spoke to her sister near the bed. She spoke of her sister Rima's shock after falling in love with a neighbor's son. The relationship lasted five years, and he managed to secure everything for their engagement. On the day when he asked his mother to prepare to ask his girlfriend's family for her hand, his mother sat with him alone and whispered so softly he could barely hear.

"Son, do you want to marry her when she is your sister?" she said.

"What do you mean, Mom? I've been with her for five years and she loves me, and no one can separate us from each other. Of course, you don't want her to be my bride. You want your niece to be my wife."

"No, my son. This is your life, and you marry the one you want, but the neighbor's daughter is your sister, and you aren't allowed to marry her!"

"Are you kidding?"

"No, my son, sit down and listen to what I'm going to tell you. You know that when Rima was only a week old when her mother died. Rima's father took her to the doctor to consult about finding the right milk for her. The doctor wrote the name of the milk, which was useful, but her father couldn't find that type. Instead, her aunt brought her to me and I breastfed her. From that day on, she became your sister by breastfeeding."

"My mother, I don't believe what you're saying, because I'm seven years older than her! How could she be my sister by breastfeeding?"

"My son, your sister was born a week before Rima. So, I breastfed them both."

His nerves collapsed, the shock so strong because of the deep love that bound Rima and him for five years. All their dreams faded because his mother called Rima his sister. He stopped eating and drinking and his health worsened.

When thinking of this story, I knew the most important thing for me was to take care of myself. I needed many things, including an up-to-date phone. I needed a mirror to see my face and life's shocks reflected in it. I'm still in my youth, and I want to see myself in the eyes of good people, and not go gray trying to be accepted by society.

I went to the house of Um Salim, who'd been asking me to work for her. I considered asking about a room for rent but first started working there. One day, after work, I hadn't finished washing the coffee cups after the fortune-telling party among unemployed women. They had no other occupation than fortune-telling sittings, which included chatting and gossiping, or going door-to-door for home visits.

After they left Um Salim's house, she repeated what the cup reader said to her and waited to interrogate her husband. She spoke the cup reader's words to him, including a message about a beautiful girl with green eyes.

"What does she want from you?" Um Salim said.

"There is no girl," he said. "I didn't move from my office, and I continued to work until I finished my shift. What is this story? Oh, Um Salim, every day you receive me with this subject instead of making a comfortable atmosphere for me. Where do you get this news? Oh, good women, every day you greet me with disturbing news."

Abu Salim entered the bedroom and slammed the door. His wife ran after him, cursing.

"Every day after you go to work, I turn a cup of coffee with your name and a cup with your mother's name," she said. "Al-Bassara Um Fouad, her reading never lies. She tells me all about you and your mother."

He rested in the bedroom before calling his wife to make lunch. He was still angry. She also seemed to have much to say while eating. Abu Salim began talking to her softly.

"Oh, Um Salim, the value of our relationship is greater than the problems that you create every day, and it is shameful that we raise our voices," he said. "I saw how Farah, the maid, looked at you when you were angry, mocking you. I wish you would read a book or a magazine to educate yourself instead of fortune reading and empty talk."

She was waiting on any word from her husband that could spark their fight again.

"Who were you with, and where did you go?" she asked.

"There is no point in talking with you," he said. "Thirty years and you have not changed anything."

He picked up his bag and walked out of the house. Um Salim immediately called her neighbor.

"I am making coffee and waiting for you," she said.

Then Um Salim called to me.

"Come, Oh Farah," she said. "It is late."

"Will you let me go, ma'am?" I asked.

"After we finish drinking coffee, you wash the cups and then go."

The cup-reading neighbor came and repeated what she'd said in the morning, adding to it some gossip that created more problems.

Um Salim added that her husband didn't treat her the way he used to treat her. He was asking her to read a book instead of having women gather for fortunes in her house. Al-Bassara laughed.

"What do you think, Oh Um Salim, to open an illiteracy course for the people of the neighborhood?" Al-Bassara said.

I hadn't seen women like this in all the houses I'd entered. They weren't even satisfied with reading the cups. They agreed to go to seers, and write magic spells so their husbands would stop liking any women except their wives. The visit ended, and Um Salim said to her neighbor: "I will wait for you tomorrow so we can go to the seer!"

I left Um Salim's house. I'd seen she had apartments available, but never asked her about a spot to live in since I thought her thinking might harm me. I checked the money the driver gave me, and I was surprised it was in dollars, a currency I hadn't used before.

I bought a fancy phone, the kind the rich have. I still had enough left to buy some provisions from the grocery store, and then went to Suad's house. Suad was surprised when she saw me carrying such a valuable phone and all the goods.

"Where did you get that from, Farah?" she asked. "I will not eat anything unless I know its source!"

"I didn't tell you yesterday what happened to me, Suad."

"You didn't tell me. You didn't even talk to me, you were busy writing."

"I will tell you what happened to me, and where the money came from. And now you will drink the most delicious cup of yerba mate from my hand, Oh Suad, the talk will be more interesting."

Suad looked at me carefully, as if flirting with me, and she seemed convinced of what I told her.

"How beautiful, attractive, and smart you are. Although nothing is wrong with work; you work as a maid, I think this work is not suitable for you. I know that circumstances led you to this like many people, Farah. I'm sorry to intrude on your private life, but why haven't you been involved with a guy with the intention of marrying him yet?"

I kept thinking about how to answer her. There were many things that I didn't reveal to her.

"Are you comfortable in your married life, Suad?" I asked.

Her anger appeared. She wiped her face with a paper tissue. She sighed from the depths of her chest.

"You know my circumstances, why do you ask me, Farah? We have been married for 15 years, and my husband is abroad. I take responsibility for the role of the man and the woman. Look at the rest of the women. Some women are happy in their married life."

"I will not deny you, Suad. Since I was 16, before displacement and suffering, I had an experience where I loved. But alas, after three years of that relationship, he began to backtrack. I was sincere in my love, and I tried many things so we could stay together, but he created many reasons for us to separate, including that I was unsuitable for married life. He said I couldn't run a house and a family in the future. Now, because of my work, in people's homes, they look at me disparagingly. I hope that the day will come when I prove to everyone that even if I go through force majeure, I will remain like a lioness and grow stronger. Now, I will search for my life partner on Facebook, what do you think? Does this way work? Did you know I'm on Facebook now for the first time?"

Suad smiled.

"This is not a solution," she said. "Be careful. Facebook is not a game. Sometimes it throws you into a maze from which it is difficult to get out."

"I know, Suad, but I am kidding. I remember Samar, who was imprisoned because of social media. I have to visit her tomorrow after I finish working at Um Salim's house. I'm going to take some clothes for her. I've seen her in front of me in her deteriorating condition. There's no doubt she needs someone to stand by her and ask her how she is."

Visiting her was enough to explain Samar's deteriorating mental and physical health.

"Who will visit you here?" I asked. "And who will defend your case?"

"No one visits me and no one defends me!"

She was very upset and didn't want to talk to anyone. I handed the clothes I had brought to the guard, who gave them to her. She didn't stand in front of me so I could talk to her, though, perhaps because she was tired. I contented myself with saying hello and left the prison.

On my way home, I started inquiring about a house to live in around town. Suad wished I would stay in her house forever, but I felt I was a burden. She worried about the children and her sick mother-in-law. All she needed was me to complete her misfortune. I asked the shopkeeper about a place to rent, but it was in a cellar. I was afraid to live there. After searching more, I found a comfortable place. Sunlight entered and there were neighbors around.

When the owner found out I cleaned houses, he began to tell me of a new job possibility. It was in the house of his acquaintance. I started collecting my furniture from Suad's house to move to my new house. She looked at me sadly.

"I will miss you, and I will keep in touch with you, Suad," I said. "I will never forget you."

"Will you still work in Um Salim's house?"

"I won't because I found another job," I said.

"If you saw her, Suad. How indescribable she looked when her son called to say his wife had given birth to a daughter. She was acting like she was offering condolences. Her anger increased because her fortune-teller neighbor had always told her that her daughter-in-law would have a boy. When Abu Salim knew that, he laughed for a long time at his wife. Then her tears shed, because of how he gloated."

***

CHAPTER 13

U nder psychological stress, I'd talk to myself: I am mentally and existentially unstable.

I wonder who to blame. The woman who gave birth to me and left me? Or, the war that killed Um Bassam and her entire family? I can no longer bear this situation. I have to search for a way to prove my identity, whether it is legal or illegal. I will try, whatever the result. Indeed, in times of war, half of society acts illegally in many ways; officials even live on scams.

What I asked for was not impossible. I just wanted an ID card that proves my existence, and the right to live like everybody else. Being an orphan, I'd never received an ID card. Without it, I could never finish my formal education, travel within the country, or even dream of applying for a passport to go elsewhere. Suddenly, an idea came to my mind that there was no way to postpone. When Um Bassam's building collapsed, they found all the bodies except for Um Bassam's daughter, Riaan. Suspicions swirled. Some figured she had been blown to minute pieces or burned. Others thought she might have been outside the house. Regardless, her death was not confirmed. I could impersonate her, I thought. I could say I am Riaan.

I knew most services had returned to town, including the Directorate of Population. I could tell them: I am Riaan, the girl whose house collapsed on her family.

If interrogated, I'd make up a lie they could believe. We were in such a mess and sometimes anything was believed. Although I hated lying, I knew sometimes people must believe their own lies.

I started considering who in the Directorate of Population could vouch that I was Riaan. I also considered what might happen if they discovered me impersonating her. I should have called Mulham and the guy who hit me with his car. I could have said I lost my ID card in the accident and told them my given name is Riaan. I thought about everything they could ask me, and tried to remember everything about Riaan clearly.

The surprise was that the office didn't check anything. I'd thought they had no problems except mine. But their problems were much bigger than mine. I came home to rest, and felt as if I had relieved a heavy burden. I would spend a quiet night free of noise and nightmares. I would wake up to a bright tomorrow and a new job. The sunlight would shine through the window, rousing me from sleep with its heat through the curtainless window. I checked my money. The following day I was going to splurge and go to a restaurant for lunch. I had the same rights as others. After that, I'd go to the market and buy a curtain and some household items.

I began thinking of things that hadn't occurred to me, like walking around the city, my country's capital, to places I'd never gone before. I could feel my existence more than ever after receiving my ID card.

Since my dream was to continue my education, I thought I should look for the right institute. I'd never learned Arabic under a formal curriculum. Only Um Bassam had taught me some of the fundamentals at an early age. Learning to read and write at a high level would be essential to pursue my dream of becoming a successful lawyer, someone who could defend women against injustice and discrimination. Men have the right to do anything. But if a woman makes a mistake, everyone is ready to penalize her. I had been trying to erase my past and the darkness created by the one who gave me life.

I remember Um Bassam's daughter going to her mother "hardana" and saying: "I can no longer bear it. My husband is cheating on me!"

"Be patient and he will take care of you more," her mother said. "Do not ask him for a divorce. Be patient for the sake of your family. Always smile at him. Try to prepare the most delicious food for him. Stomachs are the key to some men's minds. He might be one!"

Around the same time, her son Bassam went to his mother.

"My wife is sick and can no longer do the housework," he said, "and some of my friends are advising me to divorce her and marry another woman."

"No, my son," she said. "You have to support and take care of her, God is the Healer, and you will be rewarded."

Um Bassam always crossed my mind. She was wise in difficult times and had a forgiving heart. She seemed to find a solution to every problem. She'd given me advice as well.

"Oh Farah, life can teach you. It is a school where you learn a lot."

All these thoughts came to me while sitting in the Pullman headed for the capital. How excited I was, seeing the old lanes of Damascus, and smelling the scent of its jasmine, which attracts lovers from all over who meet in the gardens. Or, sometimes they meet at the famous Bakdash ice cream restaurant. You feel you are in the heart of the world, with so many coming to eat Shami ice cream, distinguished by its taste and careful preparation.

After some minutes, I arrived at the Al-Hamidiyah Market, surrounded by all kinds of beauty. I heard the pounding of ice cream falling into its containers. Time passed quickly. I didn't even feel it slipping by while wandering the streets filled with blessings of so many home-grown items. They call this capital the "Mother of the Poor," because some restaurants provide food at such a low price. Generosity is a valued trait among its people.

I finally returned home late. Before I went inside I saw my neighbor Abu Talaat, whom I didn't know well yet. I wanted to ask him about the work he'd mentioned. Where and when should I go?

The door was wide open, and my neighbor sat on a chair beside his sick wife's bed, serving her food. He showed me how to take care of his wife, who'd been paralyzed for five years. He was the only one who cared for her. The pictures of three young men on the wall caught my eye.

Where are they? I asked. So, he recalled the sorrows buried in his heart. Yet he seemed unable to describe his tragedy, tears falling. I consoled him by telling him of my difficult experiences.

His wife tried to take part in the conversation, but I couldn't understand her slurred words. Abu Talaat did tell me the location of the house that needed a maid, but then he asked me to come back after work to help take care of Um Talaat. I could also clean, wash, and cook in his house in exchange for rent.

Still, when I left I entered my room apprehensive of him. I lived alone, and there was nobody else around except him and his wife. I couldn't overcome my suspicions of any man.

I used to stay at work until 3 p.m. When I came home, I found Abu Talaat waiting for me at the door, so I could help him with housework. I asked him to leave the house until I finished, but he insisted on staying. I noticed him watching me, looking somewhat suspicious. I went to my room for a break, but he called me.

"Oh Farah, Um Talaat needs you."

I was just there shortly before, I thought, this man is strange.

"What does Um Talaat want?" I asked.

"She wants to drink herbal tea from your hand," he said.

I began tiring of this routine, so I started looking for another house without telling him. Before I could leave, Abu Talaat went too far. He knocked on my room's door in the middle of the night.

"Oh Farah, come help me with Um Talaat!"

I became angry first. Then I didn't respond until he gave up and left. His behavior spooked me, and sleep flew from my eyes that night. I opened a book, hoping it might absorb my anger. I read until the morning. When I looked out my room's window, I checked to see if any people were around. It was only Abu Talaat standing and looking at my window. Maybe he cared for me or felt sorry for me after I'd told him about my situation, yet he now restricted my freedom to work and rest as I saw fit. It seemed he acted like that because he was still suffering the loss of his children. He also needed someone to talk to. Maybe he genuine- ly liked me. Nevertheless, these reasons don't justify his actions. And I didn't find comfort in that house, whatever his intentions. I avoided him so as not to argue with him, even leaving for work surreptitiously.

Against my will, I found myself imagining being in front of my Aunt Fadia's house. Perhaps I sensed something about my mother Fuda, even while I tried to forget the past. Her story followed me like a shadow. No one can forget their mother, whatever her behavior. The child inside me still longed for my mother's arms. I looked out the window and felt indescribable emotional pain. Then, I went to work. Yet I was convinced that I couldn't calm down until hugging my mother, and I felt I knew the reasons that prompted her to leave me.

At Um Samer's house, the work that day was different from the rest of the days. Um Samer had established an association for the women of the neighborhood. She gave it a purpose, too. The association pooled together money for a loan at every monthly meeting, based on whoever had pressing needs to meet.

"Who among you needs a loan?"

Um Samer asked in their first meeting. Everyone said they did.

"I need surgery that costs a lot. Please, I want it to be my turn first!" one said.

"I need the money, because I am sick with cancer," another said. "I need medicine and its price is high."

All of them were in dire need. Um Samer was confused but suggested they draw lots. And the lucky one takes the first loan. Their voices overlapped, the women wondering who would draw the papers while they wrote their names.

After discussing, they said it should not be a member of the association. UmSamer said she had a solution. She would ask the maid Farah to draw the first paper. When Um Samer called, I rushed to them. There were about 20 women, all watching while I drew one name. In silence, each woman probably wished that the loan would be for her. I drew Um Samer's name. They turned to her in astonishment. Their looks accused me of being partial, too. We now live in a society used to cheating and bribery.

"I will give this money to Um Khalid, who is sick with cancer," Um Samer said, "because the medicine cannot be delayed, and when her turn comes, she will pay me the money."

After that, they decided to hold the next meeting in the house of Um Khalid. Later, Um Khalid spoke to me.

"Oh Farah, you have to come to my house early to help me. How much do want for one day?"

"From the moment I knew you were sick," I said. "I decided I would help you for free."

The association ended its historic first meeting, and I cleaned past dusk. I ran to my house, scared by a sound made from a trash can. I thought cats were eating leftovers. When I reached the trash, a boy raised his head from inside and cried loudly for help, saying glass shards thrown out had wounded him. He said he was bleeding. I stood confused and afraid. What could I do to help that boy? The sight of blood terrified me, and I didn't recognize him. I went on my way and felt guilty.

How could I not help him, I wondered. What would he do? Was he hungry and went into the trash for left-overs? Did glass shards in the trash really cut him? Or was he mentally ill? Or pretending so he could steal from passers-by like me?

All possibilities existed these days. There was no black and white. The colors intertwined, and I wandered off with these thoughts. When I reached the house, I heard Abu Talaat's dog bark. He had let him wander in the yard. He barked more when I tried opening the outer door, and I yelled in fear.

"Oh, Abu Talaat!"

He didn't answer. I called him on my phone but there was no answer. I couldn't enter for fear of the dog. He was like a werewolf to me. And the house was isolated at the end of town with no neighbors. Where could I go?

My friend Suad came to my mind. I missed her. I called but she didn't answer. The dog kept barking right inside the door. No doubt he wished to catch me through the slits of wrought iron. My teeth chattered from fear. Suad sent me a message saying she was leaving for a trip. Oh God, where should I go tonight? I thought.

My eyes watched the door of Abu Talaat's room. The situation was strange. He didn't hear my voice nor his dog's barking? I was wary of this old man. It kept me awake.

The dog walked away toward the door of Abu Talaat's room. I knew the dog heard a sound. When Abu Talaat came out, he opened the door to see only the dog and returned to his room, closing the door. I burst out crying. Abu Talaat came out suddenly, carrying a rope and grabbing the dog. He tied it around the dog's neck, and fixed the rope leash to its peg. Abu Talaat turned toward me.

"How long have you been here, Farah?" he asked, opening the door.

I quickly entered my room and slammed the door behind me angrily, while he murmured.

"Not even a hello?" he said. "I am wrong to tie the dog. I should have let him eat you!"

Who is this man? As if he needed to take revenge on me, even though I didn't say anything to hurt him. Maybe he was just making fun of me?

I sat to rest and browsed my phone. I thought about the association meeting. I'd moved between them to meet Um Samer's requests, providing hospitality, while I heard them quietly criticizing Um Samer about small details. One said the color of the roses did not suit the guest room.

"Look at the painting on the wall, how strange," another said. "And its placement is not appropriate."

Soon, I saw how they all were scrolling on their phones, looking at whatever caught their interest. One looked at fashion sites and showed her friends the latest. Another monitored the exchange rate of the dollar and gold, telling others about the prices. A third followed love stories, telling those around her about the success or failures of the romances.

A fourth found murders and kidnappings. A fifth read a comment written by her husband's friend, going crazy when she saw the woman replying to him with a flower emoji. A sixth checked out who got married and who got divorced. A seventh read the employment section after having completed her university education ten years ago and still job-searching. An eighth shopped the latest models of cars. A ninth looked at the latest phones. A tenth watched the news about the army's progress in the North, anxious about her soldier son. I knew this woman was a widow, through her friends, and she was looking for a new love.

I felt the lack of privacy in the group just helped them show off as they do on Facebook. Some posted what they ate at a fancy restaurant to brag, without caring that some people can't find a bundle of bread for their children. Even some of the women here didn't use social media because they were in dire financial situations. They waited their turn to buy medicine or other necessities. Their pain deepened when they heard rich people showing off their children's excellence in study.

When I read Facebook, which shares news across the whole world, I see how one does whatever they want. Some use social media wisely, and some allow it to destroy them.

All these thoughts about what I'd seen and heard that day, so I didn't realize I'd spent a long time in my room until Abu Talaat knocked. He was carrying food and drink, intending to restore his dignity.

Who is this man? He didn't come until late at night. He started apologizing and saying he didn't mean to scare me with his dog. He said he was sleeping deeply and never heard me.

"I didn't even hear my phone ringing."

"I didn't get angry with you," I said, "you are like my grandfather."

His face flushed, his eyes widened, and his mustache shook. He started saying repeatedly, "My grandfather, my grandfather!"

He'd forgotten that he was 75. The strange thing is that he spent nights awake walking in the courtyard, and I'd hear him talking to the dog a long time. He was tense whenever I'd see him, mouthing words. I'd searched for a new home, but I hadn't found the right place yet. I thought he'd begun looking for reasons to knock on my door.

"Do you need anything?" he'd ask.

One time he started talking about something I couldn't have conceived.

"I would like to protect you, Oh Farah. You are alone, you have no family, no home. I am ready to register all my property in your name. Um Talaat is in her last days."

He was asking for my hand. He paused, a little confused when I didn't respond. He stuttered on.

"Since the day I got to know you, I have been thinking about you during the day and night!"

He opened his mouth but didn't finish what he wanted to say. Then, after a long silence, he said it.

"I love you," he said.

I asked myself, How could he go so far? I am 20 years old. I didn't answer him for fear of hurting him. I was afraid of him leaving the dog without a leash.

"Fine," I said.

Then he left for his room. Perhaps he dreamed as he wanted.

In the morning, as I was going to work I watched him come home from afar.

I looked to the right and the left, trying to pass at a distance. He was smiling at me, though, and held a bag from which he took a jewelry box. He opened it, and approached me. The box held two engagement rings.

"Do you like it?" he asked.

I continued on my way laughing at how I kept moving past him. Before work, I continued looking for housing. I agreed with one home's owners about the rent without knowing details. I returned with the owner of the vehicle to move furniture, at a time when Abu Talaat would have thought I'd be at work.

Fortunately, he didn't come from his room until we'd finished loading the furniture. We were ready to leave.

He came out wearing his white galabiya and looked as if he'd just taken a bath. He put his hand over his face, looking surprised at the presence of a car loaded with furniture. He looked at the door of the room, where I'd stuck an envelope with the outstanding rent. When I reached the new house, I hoped I would be erasing my fear of that man.

***

CHAPTER 14

I t's painful that some don't have homes in their country to shelter themselves. Sometimes, they're the ones who love their country so much they can't leave it for a day. Yet they spend their lives moving from one house to another while others have everything, including freedom. While some send the country's money and goods abroad, these people have no time to think about anything but their livelihood. They find themselves a slave to others. Neighbors sometimes bring out all the beauty in them, while others destroy their souls.

Hopefully, I would get along with my neighbors this time. I had no outlet except the window in my room, which did present an amazing view of a vast garden of roses. I could see a path for lovers to wind through the garden. I watched a couple turn their eyes to the most beautiful rose. One of them bent, touched it, and inhaled its scent. Yet he still wasn't satisfied, so he picked the rose and offered it to his beloved.

And, still, the one rose was not enough. They moved throughout the garden, picking a bouquet of different colors. After they picked them, though, he knew they would wilt without water and placed the bouquet on the ground near the river bank. The couple sat on the grass there, and after enjoying a splash of the water, began throwing the roses into the river. The roses floated on the surface until disappearing. I watched in shock while trying to understand how they could pick roses meant for everyone to enjoy. I considered it an assault on the life of a being that cultivates nature.

Nevertheless, what I saw drew me into the park. I moved among the roses, where other park-goers only inhaled their scent and admired their sight. I sat on the river's edge under a tree, looking at the abundance of water. It carries the smallest pebbles and all the impurities of the soil. Flowing wildly, the sound of its gurgling became louder.

Another couple kept moving from one spot to another to escape the sun's intense heat, before settling under an old eucalyptus tree. They spoke of their childhood when they'd throw lush plants that they'd picked into the water. The woman insisted the river was clear in the past and didn't carry the impurities it carries these days.

I contemplated the river, too: How many secrets flowed with that water? How many innocent people's secrets were buried beneath its surface? How much innocent blood was swept away? How many forged papers did it drown? How many autumn leaves blew from the fields to the water? How many anemone roses bloomed in the land it waters? How many trees adorned their branches with green leaves? And how many things were washed away by the waters, sunk beneath the soil?

I wondered: Do we remember everything as beautiful, clear, and stable from our childhood? Or, have we indeed changed? This question baffled me. Each time I walked in the garden, I left with many still unanswered questions.

The scene became complete when the domestic pigeons landed on the grass, expecting visitors to scatter wheat for them. They moved around and looked left and right, but found nothing. One stood as if waiting for her peers, then flew from the garden. After a while, she returned. A young working-class man had entered the garden holding a bag. His bag was like a message, the pigeon received him. The bird fluttered about, and waited for the young man to open his bag. He scattered wheat, and several pigeons flocked and celebrated. The routine played out after his every absence and return. It reminded me of what I saw working in Abu Khalid's house. He always scattered wheat for the birds at his front door at a specific time. The flock would gather at the appointed time and wait. Some birds landed near him, while others flew to make him notice. They would continue following him as he walked to work several minutes away.

One day, a sparrow stood on the iron mesh, and knocked on Abu Khalid's door with its beak. He had been away from home for days. I didn't know how to explain that: Was the bird on a quest for food or checking in on Abu Khalid because it missed him?

I asked myself how that tame creature had a language that humans do not speak. And yet people enjoy hunting or caging them. If they watched how a mother feeds her babies, they might not do so. We used to watch those birds when we were young, flying in the sky and garnishing it with geometric shapes no humans could imitate, no matter how much they trained. With their aerials, the birds painted a lightness and happiness in our hearts. We looked at them and shouted as loud as we could, rejoicing in those shapes every autumn, as they migrated to countries with warmer climates, crossing the skies of our country as it grew cold.

These memories remind me of Um Bassam's friend, an old woman who talked about domestic birds as if they were chickens.

"At a bride's wedding," she said, "you see chickens running behind the wedding ceremony to pick up the rice, which is scattered on the bride's procession by the owners of the houses they pass. Chickens celebrate at every gathering, in particular in condolence ceremonies. A weak creature's belief follows its instinct that every gathering is sprinkled with rice!"

Hallelujah. The chicken can trade secrets with all his fellow creatures. Meanwhile, man is unable even to build the nest.

I smiled when I imagined such a miracle. It gave me some inner peace. When a bird landed in front of me, I spent my day optimistic. I had begun trying to invoke a bright hope my soul could send to my body, which was tired of being in houses I was forced to enter for my livelihood. I hoped time would pass quickly so I could complete my education and stop cleaning people's homes.

Regardless, I could not stop searching for my mother. I could not fall asleep before retreating in my memory to people whispering about me and seeing their sarcastic looks.

"Even if she is beautiful," I heard them say. "It is forbidden to look at her!"

The boys and girls used to gather to play in the neighborhood. I begged them to play with me, but their rude answer was that their mothers had warned them against it.

Several times I tried to forget this memory. Yet even if I did forget, they would not. It would remain a mark even after my death.

I focused on my work in Um Samer's house. This wise, humble woman cared about raising her children, watched over their studies, and solved the problems between her and her husband before they grew bigger. She acted and spoke with calmness and respect. Her husband also respected her.

"You, Farah, are one of the family members," she told me. "You can behave as you like at home."

Thursday was the most beautiful day for Um Samer, and she prepared the most delicious food and sweets for her children to spend Friday with her after they returned from the university. Um Samer spent the most beautiful moments with them. They told her all the details of their lives with classmates from the week. Her daughter also told her about the young man who sat next to her in the Pullman. He was showing interest by asking about her life. She asked questions that did not go beyond his work and hobbies. She smiled cunningly in response to his answers.

Then she opened a book and turned its pages to keep busy with anything until the trip ended safely, with everyone exiting and the man letting her be. She told her mother this always happened to her. Her mother said she should treat everyone with love, caution, and kindness, but be aware that some young men had a meager upbringing. She should not allow them to take their relationship far enough to make mistakes she'd regret.

Um Samer's house gave me enough comfort to continue my studies. She helped me around the house, and her children helped me when I needed a tutor. I prepared to take an exam for my secondary school certificate. When I arrived for the exam, much younger students were wondering if I was their exam supervisor.

When I sat next to one, he looked at me in astonishment and laughed.

"Are you still in the ninth grade?" he asked.

I smiled and did not answer.

I left the exam joyful, with great hope that I'd excel in the first subject.

On my way home, I passed in front of my Aunt Fadia's house. I hoped

my mother would be waiting to see me from the window. She might ask: How was your exam? She would be like the other children's mothers who wait. I looked up to the window.

I didn't pay attention when I stepped into the street. A truck loaded with gas cylinders was parked for delivery and I walked right into it, slamming my leg against its unforgiving frame.

"Look in front of you," the young driver shouted. "Why are you looking at the high windows?"

The pain shot through my leg. The young man continued saying things I didn't want to hear.

"All the girls are looking up?" he asked. "What is on high?"

He was cursing our generation, forgetting that he was the same age. My leg hurt so badly, I put most of my weight on the other leg and limped away. He offered me a ride wherever I wanted to go, telling me I could ride between the gas canisters. I told him to get out of my way and go wherever he wanted. He kept walking beside me and never stopped asking me to ride with him.

"Oh, I know why you do not accept a ride in a gas truck," he said. "You want to ride in a taxi. Where do I get this taxi from? I have not found a job that I like, even though my certificate is hanging on the wall at home."

He went on his way while he was mumbling words I couldn't hear well. He was broken and frustrated himself. I finally reached the room where I lived in, in an old house belonging to Abu Tareq. I was surprised by the wedding there, and I couldn't enter my room. Men were leaving the main door, and they stopped and waited for the bride to finish saying goodbye to her family and relatives. Her tears ran down her face, spoiling her makeup. I watched them until they accompanied the wedding procession, and fired into the air with rifles, as if they were on a battlefield. I entered my room, and her father, Abu Tareq, and her mother, Um Tareq, were still shedding tears for their only daughter's departure.

I cleaned and bandaged my wound. Fortunately, I didn't have to work in anyone's house before I finished the exam. The next day, the sounds of joy were replaced by quarrels and insults between family members. The home full of joy had turned into hell. I wondered how it was possible that happiness turned so quickly into tragedy. Their voices came from here and there until the bride reached the door of my room. She knocked on it hard.

"Open the door for me, I beg of you!" she yelled.

As I let her in, Abu Tareq and Um Tareq were coming after their daughter with sticks in their hands. I had no choice but to lock the door on them. I needed to preserve my house's sanctity.

The day before they had cried over the bride's departure. Now, she threw herself on the ground, trembling with fear and pain. She looked terrified, her eyes bulging while her face turned yellow and her body tensed. I was afraid that something bad would happen to her while she was in my house. Finally, she passed out. I soaked a piece of cotton with hand sanitizer nearby, and put it under her nose to smell. Finally, she moved. I waited until her nerves calmed, then I offered her water and moistened her dry mouth. I gave her tissues to wipe the sweat from her body.

Her father and mother were yelling outside, waiting for her. Whatever the reasons, I would not allow anyone to touch the guest in my house, even if it cost me my life.

"You must come out, Nabila," they yelled. "We are here. Where are you going?"

I began to pray.

"Oh, God. I took a break from my job to devote myself to studying. What is this? What do I do?"

I offered juice to Nabila. Still nervous, she didn't respond. I tried to reassure her.

"No one can touch you as long as you are in my house. Tell me, Nabila, what worries you so that I can help you. What happened? Yesterday was your wedding. Are you forced to marry this young man?"

Nabila could not answer. Tears streamed down her face. She soon fell asleep, and I opened my book to prepare for a math exam the following day. I fell asleep while studying. I woke up to a tapping on the door. The power was out, and it was raining steadily. Water dripping from the roof sounded like a ticking clock. Before I lit a candle, I looked out the window, afraid that someone was waiting for Nabila.

Instead, I saw a blessing. Her father and mother had returned to the house because of the rain. I lit the candle as Nabila tried to get up. I returned to my bed.

"Is anyone outside the door?" Nabila whispered.

"Nobody," I said. "The goodness of heaven made them return."

"Sit down, Farah, I want to tell you what happened so you can help me, otherwise my family will insist on killing me. I swear by God that I am innocent of everything they accuse me of. My wedding day was the dream that I was waiting for. On the second day of my engagement, my fiancé joined in flag service, and I waited for him. But because of the war, he served eight years. I was hoping that my dream night would come true, and we were very happy. But I regret every second I waited for him because my fiancé's dream was to prove his manhood with the amount of virgin blood I spilled on the wedding night. Unfortunately, the hymen was already broken. This is what the doctor said when our families went the next day. After the doctor examined me and wrote a report confirming my virginity, they were not convinced of the doctor's words. Immediately, my husband tore up the report. His mother told him rudely that I had returned to my family's house.

"What should I do, Farah? Most people think like my family and his family. If I survive, how will I face people, relatives, and society?"

"So be it," I said, "the parents act with a kind of ignorance, and there is no blame on them. The blame is on your educated husband who acts as his mother says. Here is our situation: each of us is suffering differently from the other. We have to challenge all violence, and not care about society, and what it forces, because we were raised fearing people's words, but we are right and they are wrong. Nabila, if you knew my problem from my childhood, you would know it burns inside me like embers. With all this, I lie to myself to live and challenge society. I will rise and prove my existence."

We were still talking when someone knocked on the door. Through the window, I saw Nabila's husband and mother. In surprise, I told Nabila he might have regretted what happened and came to apologize. They seemed quiet. I had no choice but to open the door. Nabila went with them to her family's house.

I stayed focused on studying for my exam the next day. I later heard that Nabila's mother took her to other doctors, all of whom proved Nabila had preserved her virginity. She obtained several reports. Also, Nabila refused to return to her husband's house, which caused her unforgettable pain. She continued telling me that despite all that, she was confused and ashamed to leave the house for fear of people's opinions and insults. Some meddle in others' privacy, and would force her to repeat an explanation with intimate details.

Her mother and father accepted the explanation, but she still felt their skeptical looks and belief that she had done something wrong. Her husband visited her family regularly to persuade her to return to his home.

She finally promised to return to the house that had been her dream. But confusion haunted her.

I am waiting for my dream to come true. I want to find my mother because her lap is the warmest, and no one can understand what state you are in better than your mother. Some women are in the same circumstance as my mother, even if the details are different. I have a neighbor with seven children, and she is in constant quarrels with her husband. This man hits her every day and treats her like a slave. On one occasion, curiosity prompted me to say: "Why do you have so many children if you both live like this? Why do you still live with him?"

"Sometimes, circumstances force us to live in humiliation and endure violence for a reason," she said. "I'm not financially independent, and my kids are a huge responsibility on my shoulders. Can I leave them in the alleys? I do not have a mother to return to the warmth of her lap. As for your question: 'How did you give birth to this number of children?' you are right, Farah. What can I tell you since you are an eyewitness? What happens between me and my husband, I feel as if I am being raped because I have no way to escape. The mother is the messenger, the children are the message, and they should not be abandoned."

I sighed deeply and turned back. I cannot forget the pain inside, and my nostalgia for my mother's bosom. This obsession distracted me from many thoughts, even from taking care of myself. At the last moment, I remembered the meeting of the women's association at Um Khalid's house, where I promised to help her.

***

CHAPTER 15

How lovely was Um Khalid's soul. With all she was suffering from her illness, she was trying to ignore it even when her condition worsened. She received guests with kindness and love, welcoming them and expressing her desire to sit with them.

"This meeting is the only outlet for us, to talk about the stress we feel, which we have been bearing for nine years," she said. "And each of us is looking to fill our time with something useful that could relieve the pain."

Just as sadness brought them together, joy also brought them together. A beautiful voice in this meeting began imitating the singer, Samira Toufic. She sang "Ya Hala," meaning the guest is the guest of God. There were musical instruments in Um Khalid's house. Her children had an oud and a darbuka, which she brought to a guest who knew how to play. Others sang as a chorus. Their cheerful voices rose in the neighborhood after such a long absence. Some had almost forgot to smile. They showed their talents and joy overtook them. Dancing, banter, and laughter filled the room, which had all been lacking during the war's sadness.

I looked at them sadly, though, because I was a maid and shouldn't share the joy. I was not even invited to share it, even though I looked forward to a joyful atmosphere. I'd wanted that all my life. Instead, I spent my time with clanking dishes. Music could nourish the soul, and my instability, because we are all human beings. We carry the same feelings even if our capabilities or social status differ.

Some, however, had replaced the sound of music with the sound of bullets. They'd replaced the rose with a sword. They'd replaced mercy with killing. I wished to be happy when I achieved my goal in life.

Even though everyone is born with a blank page, here in life the scribbling begins. Starting with the mid-wife and the visitors, and ending with the mother, the father, the school, the street, the clergyman, the man of power, and so on. When they grow up, in these stages, development with normalization begins as in any field: department, organization, etc. Even outside the country, they attract Arab minds to serve their country, and there is no time for us to think or live freely and decide our destiny by ourselves. We do not have a choice in anything. We work like slaves wherever we are, and spend our lives running after our livelihood. From here, violence begins as well as crimes. Problems between people worsen, and hunger motivates them. All of this suffering had lodged in my memory. My mother gave birth to me by force and threw me away by force. Now, I am forced to live as a housemaid.

I only woke from my trance when I heard the voice of Um Khalid.

"Oh Farah, where is the coffee? I remembered that I had put the coffee pot on a quiet burner until the end of the concert, to offer it to the guests."

The session was not only one of joy. Opinions differed, and I listened to what they said.

"The session ended and we did not see the hookah," one said. "When my turn comes in the association, the hookah will be more important than anything."

Some of them supported this idea. Yet others refused because of its possible harm.

"If we smoke it or not," said one, "it will reflect negatively on us because our men always use it, and we allow that."

"We have to combat this phenomenon," another said, "to preserve our health and the health of our children. Children imitate their parents; the boy imitates his father, and the girl imitates her mother. If we are not a good example for these generations, we will destroy them."

At the end of the association session, Um Khalid whispered in my ear.

"Would you agree to take care of a baby girl, only a few days old? She is the daughter of Maher, our neighbor. Her mother died two days after giving birth. She is the first child, and her father is unable to take care of her because of his work. He has no relatives in this town, as he was displaced from war-stricken areas. He also told me he would offer a lucrative salary to whoever accepts. Do you agree?"

"I will think and answer you later," I said.

This subject soon took over my thoughts. I would be taking care of a child who did not know her mother and trying to give her the tenderness and love she lost. At the same time, I worried raising her would awaken many of my forgotten sufferings.

I was confused and hesitant. Still, I finally decided to tell Um Khalid I would take the job. From that moment on, I imagined what my reaction would be when I hugged her for the first time. Would I be afraid? I wanted to shower her with all the love I missed from my mother. I will always remember Um Bassam giving me so much love and affection growing up. I am sure there are still some people like Um Bassam despite so many circumstances forgetting all their morals for money and other temptations.

I was browsing Facebook, waiting for Um Khalid and Maher. He came carrying the little girl. I felt like a woman in her first labor, waiting for her baby to cry. No one can take away the role of the mother. In my relationship with Um Bassam, I reluctantly called her my mother for 20 years. She deserved more than that.

Maher carried his daughter to me, his face pale. He was slurring his words due to the dryness of his mouth, and tears flowed involuntarily from his eyes. Then going out, he looked back.

"Silva is a little angel," he said. "I will not vouch for her to you again. She is a trust in your lap, and I will talk to you every day on the mobile phone to check on her, and during my vacation, I will come and take her home with me to spend my days with her."

Um Khalid would be my guide to know what Silva needed, in terms of milk and medicine. Silva was fast asleep for now, but I was anxious to wake her up and hug her.

***

CHAPTER 16

I delayed the housework and sat next to little Silva. I watched her fall into a Ghazlani sleep with eyes slightly open. Her eyes housed divine beauty, her eyelashes thick and dark as if eyeliner dripped from her eyes.

I did not fall asleep for fear Silva might wake up. Soon, Silva yawned. She moved her head left and right, opening her mouth in search of her mother's breast.

How happy I would have been to breastfeed her. She'd lost this maternal connection like I did as a baby, but I still hoped to find my mother. While feeding her with a milk bottle, I whispered.

"Do you know what the difference is between you and me, Silva? When you grow up, you will know that you have lost your mother, which is your destiny. Your father did not abandon you and he provides you with a life of comfort. But my mother is still alive and I have not seen her. That is why I die every day many times by what people say about me. And I do not know who my father is."

I talked as if she could understand what I was saying. I often complained about my worries, as if she were a priestess relieving my pain. Silva's only challenge was that she feared the dark whenever the electricity went out. She screamed. I picked her up and talked to her. She still trembled. I lit the candle and she calmed a little, looking at me as if I were the one in total control of light and darkness. I couldn't convey to Silva the idea of rationing electricity, and how she must adapt to it.

"Don't you know where you are?" I said. "Of course, if you knew, you would not have accepted this life. You are in a world that has changed a lot. Where there is no mercy. Some became like wild beasts. The strong eat the weak, and there is no honesty or logic. Everything became immoral. Silva, I hope to see you when you grow up, and I hope you will be strong as a lioness!"

I wanted to take Silva to visit my neighbors whom I hadn't seen for a long time. I usually loved to visit, but I came home with regrets. As soon as I entered their house, they looked at me suspiciously.

"Who is this child?" they asked. "Since when?"

I explained Silva's situation. They looked at each other and whispered, not believing what I was telling them.

"I have been hearing her crying for some time, and I am surprised," one of the women said. "I wondered where this voice comes from knowing that you live alone, Farah. The saying goes: 'The girl becomes like her mother.'"

I asked myself, Who told her the news of my mother that I have kept secret? She continued sarcastically and rudely.

How beautiful, I thought, to live your life with an innocent child. You don't have to mix with people who try to steal your inner strength. I spent time with Silva without complaining or getting bored.

In the ensuing years, I saw her grow like a flower. I loved her more every day. I took her to the park. In the fresh air, she soon walked. Then she ran, sometimes among the roses, fluttering like a butterfly from one flower to the next. Other times she sat on the ground, picking grass or scraping the dirt with her little fingers. I watched closely to make sure she didn't put it all in her mouth. When Silva saw a bird landing near us, she'd try to catch it. She'd look at the bird and run. The bird flew while Silva fell to the ground. I lived her joy moment by moment. I held her to my chest and kissed her, feeling like she was a part of me.

I brought her home once she'd become exhausted. I bathed her, while talking and singing. Before she fell asleep, I promised her that next time she could ride on the swing like the other children.

I gave Silva things she could take to her father's house. His time off was approaching, and he would no doubt come to take her home with him. In her absence, my house lost the beauty she'd added. I'd lost something I'd been searching for all along. Her presence had given me security. I would miss her to the point of distraction. I began thinking about whether I'd be able to separate from her when she turned three years old, which was the agreement with her father. I couldn't imagine. How would I give her up?

When her father came to pick up Silva, he spoke about his improvement both psychologically and physically, continually trying to heal after the devastating loss of his wife.

"Life did not stop for anyone," he said. "I will continue being optimistic and trying to bring joy to Silva to compensate for the loss of her mother's affection."

He held Silva on his lap and she leaned forward toward me. Sometimes, she wanted to go with him.

Other times she didn't. In those painful moments, she reached out her hands and begged me to stay with her. Her father's gaze toward me changed. I could sense many emotions in those looks. Once, he said, "Farah will come with us!"

Then, he became flustered, looking at me and trying to say he was just teasing Silva. That bothered me. I wanted to believe it wasn't just a ploy to calm Silva down. I had a feeling I'd never experienced before, as if warm water flowed over my body. I thought about whether he was seriously thinking about it. He wouldn't think of me as well-educated. But could he forget I was a maid and had just received my basic education certificate?

My imagination drifted from the reality I lived in, flying to another space. At least I had the right to dream about what would make me happy. Although I wasn't convinced I wanted to commit to anyone, feelings sometimes caused me confusion, hesitation, and an inability to focus on Silva. My memories carried me back to my life story and my mother, whose voice I wished I could hear. My mother filled my dreams, and also woke me up to pay attention to my studies and take care of myself.

One day, Um Tariq, my neighbor, knocked on the door. We hadn't seen each other for a while. I explained the story of Maher and his daughter. She told me about the possibility of working abroad as a maid for a lucrative salary.

"I'm not tempted by money," I said. "I'm happy working in my country, and this is a temporary profession. I'm taking courses to complete my education. Thank you, though."

Um Tariq didn't comment on my decisive answer, and left after finishing her coffee. I hoped to be around someone who supported my ideas on improving my life. Oddly, most people don't like change.

My cell phone rang late one night. Maher apologized for the time, but said he needed to speak with me.

"Silva is still crying and not sleeping, and I do not know what she's complaining about. I'm very worried about her!"

I said he should boil anise for her. The cold might be causing her anxiety. I worried about Silva, too, thinking she missed sleeping on my lap. In bed, I tossed and turned, hearing her cries. I was in pain because of her pain. In the morning, I woke up still tired. Maher returned with Silva, who threw herself at me. I carried her while she clung to my neck. Her father looked concerned and confused. She was supposed to stay with him that day, but he said she had not calmed down all night or fallen asleep. I reassured him not to worry, and told him I would call if needed.

"Silva, look at me, I am going," he said.

She was still holding me close, and tightening her grip around my neck. She didn't look at him.

"How will this child live without a mother?" he said.

After Silva was sure her father had left, she got off my shoulder. She closed the door and looked as if she were telling me her father would not come back. She found her toys around the house, and put them in front of me so we could play. I spent all day playing with her, feeding her, singing her to sleep, and stroking her silky golden threads of hair.

When you feel the inner child within you, living the innocence of children again with play, you are making them happy while you feel happy, too.

I happily bore the responsibilities of helping raise her. I saw what was happening in the world around us, with blame always falling on the mother. She was always the one responsible for her daughter's reputation, even if a mistake is beyond a mother's control, no one took mercy on her. They accompanied her to the grave with harsh words. Meanwhile, no one blamed the father. I told Silva I hoped she remained in my care until she headed off to university.

I remembered Um Bassam talking to the neighbors when I was little. She looked at me as if I didn't understand what she was saying. But I was paying attention to what they said. I learned my mother, Fuda, had also lost her mother. After my mother's mother died, her father remarried. His new wife didn't raise my mother well or with tenderness.

"Fuda would come from school, and find no one in the house, and all the doors of the house locked," Um Bassam said. "Her father was always at work, and his wife wanted to go around the neighborhood and get acquainted with everything. She'd spend her time outside the house, and not return until her husband had returned home.

"Sometimes, Fuda would be sitting outside the house in the cold or heat until her stepmother returned. Sometimes her stepmother did not come, so she would go to one of her friend's homes to eat with them if she was hungry. She often went to school in the morning without food and without good hygiene."

So begins the story of loss, which my mother suffered in absence of spiritual nourishment from her mother. Nobody compensated her with what was as important as food and drink.

At 20 years old, I now understood the meaning of the conversations between Um Bassam and her friends.

All these thoughts came to my mind as I continued my work at home until Silva woke up. I was so attached to her because she'd also lost the nourishment of her mother's soul. The mother is the foundation of the house, and the one who fills it with love, tenderness, and everything beautiful.

I'd like to nurture this innocent child. One child seemed to take up all my time. I'd ask myself, How do mothers give birth to ten or more? How much she must suffer from physical and mental fatigue? How can she meet all their requests over her own needs? Does she feel like a human being created only to give birth, raise, and bear all this burden?

Often, I was asked: "Why don't you get married, Farah, like the rest of the girls?"

Some believed I didn't get married because I had issues. Indeed, they were right! I was afraid to get married. Scared? Yes, scared! I wasn't afraid of responsibility. Rather, I was afraid to choose a man who was not right for me and discover that after it was too late. I might have married a man who did not fear God. He might have seen me as a body at night and a maid during the day.

I was afraid of a cold-hearted man who knew nothing of love except living under one roof.

I was afraid of someone who wouldn't value me or allow me to speak. Some men believe women are deficient in intelligence.

I was afraid of a man who would curse and make fun of my writing and preferred to spend most of his time with his friends in cafes.

I was afraid of a man who liked to dominate and control my freedom.

I was afraid of a man who teased me because I worked in people's homes.

I was afraid of an unknown future for my children. What if they were displaced here and there?

Perhaps I was different from other girls. My life story planted fear and confusion in me.

I was more afraid when I remembered my mother.

I needed a psychiatrist. Everyone was afraid of the anxiety and dread around them. There was nothing to reassure them because of the conflicts, crises, and epidemics.

Many people did not realize that you could have a heart that accommodates the entire world. You have ambitions you would like to achieve before it is too late, and you have a thousand scenarios for the beginning of your love story. You have many principles on which you would like to raise your children. No one can stand and shout against this world, asking for help to stop this disaster and leave you room to live without worry and fear. The war had made everything endangered.

I finished my work and Silva woke. Still, my thoughts did not stop. I wrote them with my pen. Only my pen heard and listened to me. It understood and didn't debate, blame, or mock me. My pen belonged to me without restricting my freedom.

Here the problem began. How do I give Silva a cold meal of milk when the temperature is below zero? In what way can I explain to her the reasons behind the power cuts, lack of fuel, the cold, the ice, and so on. She was screaming from hunger and did not realize all of this. She had to wait until the electricity came on.

The ugliness of war was indescribable. A baby, a sick person, or an old woman or man does not matter?

My time with Silva was growing short, and I had to prepare her belongings. Her father was coming to take her to her aunt's house during his vacation. Silva went with her father, waving her little hand at me, and promising to come back tomorrow. She did not realize her father's vacation was for a week.

Without her, I could not sit. Everything became gloomy. I had no choice but to look for a job to relieve my loneliness. I asked Mulham if he could secure a job for me, and he immediately gave me the phone number of a man named, Abu Raed. Mulham informed me that only Abu Raed and his wife lived in the house. They did not need me for much time. Yet he'd said that Um Raed's mood was very volatile, and I'd have to get used to her.

I went out the next morning, a cold winter day, rain, and a breeze stinging to the bone. In front of a used clothing store, I asked about the price of a coat. I almost collapsed when the salesman told me 30,000 pounds. What if it was new? Poor people spend the winter without a coat and die. Why? Because they are poor?

I was surprised to meet Mulham on my way. Despite the extreme cold, he spoke of his longing for me. I couldn't believe it. I knew he was going to get into a deeper topic. He only remembered me when I needed him. I knew he lived life carelessly. I reluctantly put up with his conversation. He invited me to have breakfast with him in a nearby restaurant. Then, we would go to Abu Raed's house. He whispered that he had something to tell me. I accepted his invitation only because I had not eaten za'atar manakish for a long time. I was not fond of sitting with him. He told me he had separated from his wife. Of course, he said he was an angel with her. His wife was the problem.

Also, he blamed me for not agreeing to marry him. I ate and barely listened to what he said. I soon regretted accepting his invitation. His insistence on marriage proved his selfishness and fragility. I could not even accept him as a friend. I left to go on my way to Um Raed's house.

***

CHAPTER 17

An old woman on the balcony signaled for me to enter the house. "Is this the house of Abu Raed?" I asked.

"No!" she answered. "Who are you? Do you love him? Get out of here, today is my wedding. I am Abu Raed's bride!"

I was surprised. Mulham had told me she suffered mood swings, but he didn't say she had Alzheimer's. Yet my urge to help this poor old woman pushed me forward. I figured she had suffered many troubles in life, which led to her dementia. Her husband appeared after hearing what she'd said.

"Go ahead, my daughter," he said.

I introduced myself, and he welcomed me.

"We only need you for a week, but day and night until my daughter returns from travel," he said. "She always takes care of us."

Abu Raed started talking to his wife.

"Farah will take care of you this week. She will feed you, and wash you."

"Do you want to marry her?" Um Raed shouted at him.

Abu Raed spoke to calm her, trying to soften her delirium. He told me she'd completely lost her memory. I worked the first day without speaking much to her. I observed her behavior. Even when I fed her, she would cry sometimes. Other times she would laugh. Other times curse. Other times stop eating. Other times hug and kiss me.

She would spend her days walking around the house as if looking for something she could not find. Darkness let her imagine strange things, especially the shadows. Sometimes I fell asleep exhausted and woke terrified when she removed the bedcover.

"Who is this man who sleeps next to you?" she asked.

I slept alone and doubted anyone had entered the house. I looked all over fearing an intruder. Nothing. I spent much of the nights awake. I listened to her walk around the house, as she had not slept either. The sun finally rose.

Abu Raed's prayers for his children, who were abroad, drew my attention. He wanted to see them live well, and have no harm befall them. His wife, meanwhile, did not remember her children's names.

One time when I gave her food, she threw it in anger for seemingly no reason. She said she was not hungry, before a moment later complaining she was hungry. She said I was stingy with food.

Um Raed's elderly neighbor visited her one day. I heard Um Raed saying she was hungry, and complaining to her neighbor we were not feeding her. Her neighbor believed what she was saying and started complaining to Abu Raed.

"This maid does not feed or take care of Um Raed," she said. "You have to find another maid to take care of her."

Abu Raed shook his head.

"From the first time Farah saw Um Raed, she has known how to deal with her condition. But you have been watching her for a year in the same condition, and on every visit, you try to give us your observations. Please leave us alone. She's my wife and I know her."

When I called Um Raed to take a shower she'd argue that she'd shower a short time ago. Yet if I acted calmly enough, she entered the bathroom. I washed her body with a loofah and soap, while singing to her as if she were a little girl. Sometimes she became happy. Other times sad. Sometimes, she entered the bathroom shortly after we'd left and asked to take a shower. She was not convinced she'd just washed a few minutes ago.

Once, she entered Abu Raed's room angry and asked about the date of their wedding. Abu Raed was going along with her illogical questions, smiling.

"We are waiting for our children to arrive from their travels so that they can dance and be happy with us," he said.

She rejoiced and hurried to the wardrobe, searching for a floral dress from the days of her youth. She took off her clothes and changed into the ones she had chosen, preening before the closet mirror.

Soon, though, I faced a far bigger problem than her time-traveling. I had been busy in the kitchen. As far as I knew, Abu Raed was sitting on the balcony of the house, paying attention to his wife. When I later went to look for Um Raed, I didn't find her or her husband. Abu Raed couldn't leave the house without telling me. I thought maybe they'd gone for a walk. I went on with the housework.

My concern grew when they didn't return. I stopped everything and walked outside to look. On my way, I met Abu Raed returning with bags of vegetables from the market. He was surprised by my panic. I told him I thought Um Raed had left the house with him. He handed me the bags and went looking for her.

I returned home with the vegetables and checked to make sure Um Raed was not hiding somewhere in the house. I only saw her clothes scattered across the bedroom floor. She'd gone out wearing the lacy clothes of her youth. Then I left again to search. I remembered how she would regularly put clothes in a bag and say she was going to her family's house. Her parents died a long time ago, yet she insisted on going. Abu Raed was still trying to convince her that none of her family still lived. He would take her hand and they would visit the old home to see that they recognized nobody there. She would calm down when returning, but still had never stopped asking for her parents.

Finally, I saw Um Raed on the street. A man held her hand and asked, "Where are you going?"

He'd never seen me before in that neighborhood but I still took hold of her other hand. I thanked him for bringing her close to home.

"Who are you? How do you know her?" he asked.

I introduced myself. He blamed me for neglecting her. While we talked, Abu Raed came.

"I brought her back from in front of her family's old house," the man said. "She was walking on the old winding road."

At that time, many questions confounded me. How was her memory of so many other things completely erased? She couldn't remember her children, whom she carried in her womb. Yet she remembered her parents and the home where she grew up. At 90 years old, she'd walked to the road of her childhood.

My own longing and nostalgia had flowed in my blood for years. Its fire burned within at all times. My mother's story was never absent. She was the obsession that did not leave me. I tried to forget but could not. She was in my head, a sweet dream both night and day. Without this dream, all other dreams were nightmares.

Weekdays passed, and I was alert like a soldier. I counted the remaining hours for Silva to return to my care. One night, I checked my cell phone and saw more than a dozen missed calls from her father. When I called Maher, he said he hadn't stayed the whole week at his sister's house. Silva had not adapted to her aunt's house and was always asking for me.

"Where are you now, Farah?" he asked. "I did not find you at home."

I told him about struggling with Um Raed and said I'd now returned home. When Silva and her father arrived, she hugged me and stayed close, fearing her father would take her from me. Still, she looked at me, crying, as if blaming me for being the reason she'd gone away.

Her father seemed very tired. He asked for coffee, and looked at me while sipping from his mug. He kept completely silent and lit a cigarette. He exhaled dark smoke that spread in the room with an extraordinary intensity.

I had the feeling I understood what he felt without speaking. He was very distressed about Silva, who couldn't live without me. Yet he had no courage to propose marriage to me even though he'd already told his daughter I would come live with them. I believed the difference in social status was the obstacle. Even if he was convinced of me being a match, he was afraid of people's opinions. How could he marry a maid? If he knew the rest of the details about my story and my suffering, and that I'd begun working to improve my standing, maybe it would change. I could forget it. Yet would other people's views and their ridicule ever be left behind?

I would have never expected I'd consider going from a maid to a wife to satisfy his daughter's wish.

I did admire him and believed he was different from many others. He'd remained faithful to his wife, who died nearly three years ago, by not marrying. Others I knew would have married less than a month after their wife's death, as if replacing a piece of furniture.

Maher left in nervous silence, cigarette in his mouth. Around then, I began counting how many days remained before Silva would turn three and leave my house. The days passed so quickly. And, for me, the secondary school exam approached. I needed to stay up late to study. Some days, I felt so stressed I needed to leave the house with Silva to breathe in the air and regain balance.

***

CHAPTER 18

My daily plans stopped after COVID-19 became a global pandemic, and we were under quarantine. Maher called me to explain its seriousness, fearing his daughter could be infected.

When we are afraid we become obsessive. I'd wash my hands, then come back to repeat it moments later. Even in the war's ninth year, neither the markets nor the streets were disrupted. Life continued normally. Now, though, the aspirations of young men and women stopped. A wedding celebration was postponed, and no one knew for how long. Others who'd been preparing to graduate until the universities closed their doors. And those who'd planned to travel for work after completing years of military service, were stuck.

I was lonely. Silva's presence did compensate for many things, as I almost lived as a mother. The hugs I'd missed from my mother, I delivered to Silva. God sent her to me so I did not forget the meaning of motherhood. Some women believe motherhood is when a woman gives birth to a child. On the contrary, it is anyone who bears responsibility and cares about raising children well.

I asked myself: How did I learn the lessons that gave me strength and self-confidence? Mothers and fathers taught their children to treat me as an outcast in the neighborhood. I can't forget those days. Yet it enabled me to sharpen what I saw. The law, intended to safeguard the woman, often fails. Instead, it frequently holds her accountable for the crimes committed against her rather than protecting her as it should. How many crimes are women the victims of? A girl is killed by her brother or father, and they claim she was killed by a stray bullet. The crime happens to preserve the family's "honor," and authorities do not care to find the perpetrator. May the people abide by the legal rule, which was issued only recently, insisting on punishing those who commit an "honor" crime.

Many families have been separated by real hardship, migration, or conflicts. The war cost us many of our dreams, and nothing seemed to matter anymore. Now, notebooks became even more full of thoughts inspired by suffering, moving from the bitter time of war to the deadly time of the Coronavirus.

Someone gave me a notebook and said to me: "Read it carefully, it is copied from an unknown author."

Inside, it read:

Suddenly and out of the blue. We slept in one world and woke up in a different one.

Suddenly, Europe is no longer a dream of immigration.

America is no longer the strongest country.

Paris is no longer romantic.

New York is no longer exciting.

The Wall of China is no longer fortified.

And Makkah and Medina have no worshipers.

All mosques became deserted; even the churches closed their doors, and everyone was terrified of death. The greatest priority became securing oxygen and ensuring its availability in the event of contracting the virus.

The world has become more pure and beautiful without us. I think the pandemic was a message from heaven telling us, "The water, sky, and air without you are fine and the world continues without you. And when you come back to life, never forget that you are guests. You are not, masters of the earth. You are just guests."

I remembered Um Saleh's previous call, telling me she'd returned from travel before the quarantine. She said she missed me. I missed her very much as well. How could I see her, though? I felt like I needed to somehow. I was driven by reminiscence and love for that wise woman. I remember how she reacted when she found out the story of my life. She was the only one who gave me positive energy, with her different perspective, and loved me unconditionally. With great caution, I answered her invitation.

I wanted to express my love for her by hugging and kissing her, but COVID kept us at a distance. It was heartbreaking to stand before someone I loved without being able to touch her. Even when expressing emotions, there was an underlying sense of disappointment. Um Saleh's smile and expression matched the feelings I held for her.

Um Saleh told me about her journey and the joy reuniting with family. While I tried patiently waiting for her to finish talking about her children, I was eager for her to recall her promise to inquire about my mother through her friend in Dubai. I anxiously hoped she had some happy news.

After a long silence, Um Saleh looked at the ground. Her hands shook from nerves. Then, she looked at me as if there was unpleasant news about my mother.

"What's wrong, Um Saleh?" I asked.

"Oh Farah, in this time, nothing remains the same. The days change like the seasons of the year. We will experience moments of warmth, similar to summer, as well as cold moments resembling the stormy days of winter. People may change and leave our lives like falling leaves in autumn. However, there will also be beautiful and bountiful times reminiscent of spring. Your experiences prepare you for the future. I would like to deliver good news to you, Farah. I do not like having to tell you that your mother, Fuda, moved with her daughter to Europe because of what people were saying about her. This is what her friend who lived close to her told me."

"Aunt Um Saleh, I've prepared for everything," I said, "but it seems like I'm searching for clarity in unclear circumstances. I will try to distract my thoughts from my mother, accept her move, and focus on myself and my future."

I continued telling her that life had taught me perseverance and clarity. Little saddened me anymore because I'd reclaimed my well-being. Nobody had saved me but myself. By making myself a priority, I'd understood myself better. I'd determined my goals, and needs, and avoided being dragged behind by outdated customs and traditions. I was responsible for my thoughts and behavior.

"I will delight in all that is beautiful, like a butterfly among roses and a bee among flowers," I said.

Yet I could not get rid of my confusion. Whether I stayed as I was now, or forgot the past, people in our society would not forget who Farah was. Still, I couldn't deny how much I missed the neighborhood I grew up in, as well as my friends, even though we'd drifted apart. I didn't blame them, but I blamed their parents for teaching them to mock me.

"Farah, I have high hopes for you," Um Saleh said, interrupting my thoughts. "You know how to let go of everything that bothers you, and you know how to lead your life towards what makes you happy. You don't dwell on the past in a negative way. How happy I am with your unexpected visit today. It's great that you came to visit me, as I've been waiting for you. I wanted to call you a month and a half ago when I returned from my trip. Due to quarantine, I haven't seen any family members. Tonight, everyone has decided to gather at my place, and I'd like you to stay. Since I'm alone, I could use some company and entertainment. You will join the family gathering with my relatives. Let's make this evening lively and fun as always. I may be older now, but don't underestimate me. I'm still full of energy and I love to bring happiness to those around me. We'll spend the evening in the open-air garden."

Even though it was late April and the air was chilly, the lively atmosphere, guests along with their children, provided warmth. Conversations revolved around the suffering in quarantine, soaring expenses, gas shortages, and more power outages. And then there was the chaos, kidnapping and theft even during the day. Um Saleh stood leaning on her cane.

"Even after traveling and returning, the conversations have not changed," she said. "The problems are still the same, but the worries are worsening and gray hair is appearing prematurely."

"What is wrong with you, Um Saleh?" one man said. "All of your children are in the Arabian Gulf and you are well off, God bless you!"

Um Saleh stood. She pounded her cane on the ground with force.

"You, Abu Mahmoud, do not work like my children," she said to him. "Their life is work. Every day they work until the end of the night. While you drink your coffee all day long."

"There is no work anymore," Abu Mahmoud said. "And since the coffee price has risen, we no longer drink it."

"Um Saleh will solve all the problems tonight," another man said, "and impress us with forming an imaginary ministry, as long as the officials do not respond to you. She knows who would be suitable for each position, as she is the oldest and the wisest."

Um Saleh waved her cane in the air.

"I agree, provided all of you assume the responsibility of your position, solve problems, and govern yourselves first. Do not be like those who drive cars with tinted glass as if you don't care about anyone. And should I see you pretending not to see me, don't forget who appointed you for your position."

"We beg you, Oh Um Saleh," one of the wives said, "to support women in this ministry."

"Yes, this is good," Um Saleh said. "We hear the voices of women. If they do not demand their rights, they should not expect men to give them their rights. Men naturally love power, and women, in their view, are only good for children. It is their responsibility to give birth, raise the children, keep house, and cook.

"You, Abu Mahmoud, are the Minister of Endowments. No comment? You are a religious man. Later, I will appoint an assistant for you from one of the men. Women are not appropriate for this position."

Someone intervened before she could move on.

"My brother, Abu Mahmoud, the endowment funds are entrusted to you and they are meant to be used for the benefit of the underprivileged," they said. "These resources should not be used for personal gain or private projects."

"This talk reminds me of the time I caught Abu Mahmoud in the chicken coop while he was stealing eggs," Um Saleh said. "I think he repented afterward."

"Um Saleh, you still remember?" Abu Mahmoud replied. "That was my childhood days."

"You have no right, Oh, Um Saleh," someone else said. "You knew about this regarding Abu Mahmoud and yet appointed him as a minister? Could you not find anyone else as a cleric?"

Um Saleh couldn't be stopped.

"Abu Jadaan is the Minister of Transportation. You care about the roads more than anyone else. God bless you! You do not need someone to advise you.

"As for Nayfeh, I will appoint her Minister of Health, as she knows all those who suffer from ophthalmia, whooping cough, and joint pain. She also knows how many women are pregnant, and how many months until they give birth. They told me she was looking for a cure for Corona. She knows how to cure people or send them to the mercy of their Lord, or at least she can show Azrael the way to them."

She paused and turned toward Nayfeh: "You can also counsel the wives who are causing distress to their husbands, too."

An atmosphere of joy prevailed and their laughter rose. It had been held inside due to the quarantine's isolation.

"Tell Abu Sakher, I will appoint him as Minister of Interior," Um Saleh said about a friend who wasn't there. "He is the only one who has a file for everyone, even those who are still in their mother's womb. He is our chief and knows the ins and outs of everything, there is no objection to him!

"I will also appoint Shukria as Minister of Education, due to her exceptional skills as a teacher. She has the potential to significantly influence our children's education. However, this appointment comes with the condition that she permits teachers to maintain discipline in the classrooms, as the fear of authority seems to be lacking in students nowadays. Additionally, I propose a return to the traditional curriculum, as the contemporary one appears to have led to shortcomings."

"Our mouths are parched," Abu Mahmoud interrupted. "When will we have dessert? Um Saleh, do you plan on serving dessert?" "

"Yes, but only after I've chosen someone to take on the role of Electricity Minister," Um Saleh said. "This is a priority for me. Who do you think would be a good fit for this position?"

"Currently, there's no one suitable for the role," Abu Jidaan said. "There's no need for an Electricity Minister because our homes have no electricity. We've returned to using kerosene and Babur gas, which is a blessing. Um Saleh, you've been delaying dessert. Maybe in another gathering, you'll have completed appointing your future ministry."

But Um Saleh wanted to say something else before dessert.

"I was going to appoint a Minister of Justice, but as long as there is no injustice or aggression against anyone, the world is fine," she said. "So, I dismissed the idea."

"No one asks for a judge," Abu Mahmoud said. "Each person takes his right in his own hand. We are true men and with one shout can frighten the people who trespass against us; and if they kill one of us, we will kill two of them!"

"Watch out for me, Sheikh," Um Saleh said. "Every minister among you works hard for his children to inherit his position. Life does not last for everyone. Another thing I want to say, each one of you has to respect others, not harass women, and treat your wives well."

All this time I sat in absolute silence, listening and enjoying. Suddenly in a loud voice, Um Saleh called me.

"Oh Farah, bring rice with milk and dumplings. Once the food comes, the government and the masses will fall apart!"

Um Saleh stood.

"All evening you have been talking about the high prices," she said angrily to Abu Mahmoud. "How much did you spend on your son Mahmoud's wedding? May God make him happy. I received the news that half the food was wasted. If you'd donated it to those in need, you would have earned a reward from the Lord of the Worlds; surely everyone who filled their stomach with your food did not praise you on their way out."

"Everyone who attended the wedding and ate was happy," Abu Mahmoud. "You are the only one who directs such an accusation against me."

"I did not attend the wedding," she said, "but I echo the sentiments of those who were there to celebrate the joyous occasion with you."

"At every wedding, people like to gossip. Oh, Um Saleh!" he said.

The evening would have still ended well, but one individual who wasn't appointed a role appeared to be disgruntled and began muttering to himself. As he left, he said in frustration, "Who will address your concerns? The one seated in authority has no connection to this chaos."

Nevertheless, Um Saleh bid him and the rest farewell with a warm smile, expressing her delight over the wonderful evening they'd spent together. She kept teasing them on their way out, too.

"Don't presume yourselves as high-ranking officials, hidden from the public eye," she said. "Do visit me frequently."

After everyone left her house, she looked at me with a big smile.

"Did you like the evening, Farah?" she asked.

"It was beautiful with good people," I said.

"But I always feel like our society wastes everything. Even time."

"I do not understand what you mean, Farah!"

"I mean, if every person took care of himself, and worked hard to improve his condition, society would be well."

"Oh, Farah. They are all unemployed, and no one listens to their voice. They are looking for a place to express their opinion."

CHAPTER 19

I'd returned home two days earlier, but Silva remained with her father. How much I missed her. This child is the most beautiful thing in this world, I thought. When we reunited, her father shocked me.

"My daughter will turn three by the end of this week with you," Maher said. "I want to thank you, Farah, for the kindness and affection that you have shown her."

For me, even this compliment was difficult to handle. The situation was complicated. I held back tears. As Silva clung to me, I hugged and kissed her. She burst into tears. She wrapped her arms around my neck with a warm, childish hug.

"I will not go with you, Baba," she said. "I will stay here with Farah!"

Maher started to calm her down.

"Tomorrow we will celebrate your birthday with Aunt Farah," Maher said. "I will bring you cake and three candles, and you will blow them out."

Maher could not hide the sadness from his eyes. He'd been deprived of his wife, who'd left him this beautiful child. Silva would always remind him of her. Silva had calmed down some.

"What do you think should be the solution, Farah?" Maher asked.

The question was hard to answer. When seeing my silence, he answered his own question.

"I would like Silva to stay with you until we find someone who will care for her full-time."

I exhaled the deep breath that had been suppressed in my chest. I smiled and tears of sadness became tears of joy. It would be better if Silva always stayed with me. How much would she relieve the challenges of working as a housekeeper? I often found it unbearable, scrubbing away the dirt in a woman's home as she would sit idly, her legs raised in my presence. She cared nothing about my labor. She wouldn't spare a moment to move, even when I was cleaning the very spot she occupied. Instead, she was absorbed in her phone, scrolling through social media, living a virtual life. All the while, her children were left in the care of the nanny, who took on all their needs—from food to hygiene. Their mother would only leave the house in the evening, once she was certain her children were asleep, and then return in the morning as they were waking up. I often wondered, how many children are missing out on their mother's affection? While their mother might be physically present she's emotionally absent. At that moment, I was consoling myself. My mother's guilt must be lighter than this woman's. Her children were in front of her, and she never cared for them. I wondered when the children would feel tenderness from their mother. What will happen to them in the future? Who will they remember more: their mother or nanny?

As for Silva, she kept asking when her father would bring her the cake he'd promised the day before. She insisted going onto the balcony to wait for her father and the moment of joy. She told me how she'd blow out the candles, and that she was getting big. She'd be even bigger the next day, she said. She came back inside and put on my high heels. She wobbled right and left, and then fell to the ground. Still, she assured me that she had gotten big. Silva began describing what she'd wear when she was old enough for kindergarten and imagined how she would carry her school bag.

Later, she asked me to sit next to her on the bench outside until her father arrived. I believed there was no difference between the young and the old except for what they dream about. Young children dream of candy and dolls and clothes. Adults' dreams are in vain, the past does not return. In our time, full of tragedies, adults try to ease the burdens of life that are controlling them. War and pandemic. They spread everywhere. In addition, they imposed sanctions on us with the Caesar's Act. The government's corruption and illegal acts grow and flourish, inflicting havoc on the country.

With all that is happening, I still planted basil on the balcony, which is caressed by the daytime breeze. And I stole hope when I saw a flower blooming. I searched in the ashes for wheat like a bird hovering above. I stayed patient and hopeful.

The future had become unpredictable. Youth found themselves overcome by hopelessness. Even simple things had become challenging, such as the procuring of a ring by a young man for his fiancée. The implementation of the Caesar Act had ruined the hopes of many intending to return to their homeland. My thoughts were coming and going while watching Silva, as she had been shouting whenever seeing a man from afar: "Baba come." But the time passed and Maher did not come.

Silva did not give up hope and waited for her father until she fell asleep. All night she was talking in her sleep. I was surprised Maher did not come. He had always been on time. Perhaps there was an emergency. Two days passed, and he did not answer my calls on his cell phone. His mobile went directly to voicemail, presumably switched off. We imagined many possibilities for his absence. I would have liked to inform the authorities to search, but I was the unofficial nanny for his child. Without being a family member or spouse, or having any legally binding relationship, I didn't hold a role that allowed me to do so.

I had feelings that I didn't reveal to anyone, even to Maher. I waited for him as Silva waited for him. She waited for cake and candles. I waited for a person I'd drawn into my life, into my heart, with all my senses. I hid a glow in my heart from him. Yet confusion and hesitation in dealing with men made me unable to figure it all out.

I tried going to bed early but could not sleep. I spent the night tossing and turning, playing with Silva's hair. I hoped that she would wake up, and amuse me. The night was so long as I waited for dawn. I envied Silva for her sound sleep.

My soul awakened when I saw the sun's rays around me. I rose from bed, and brought a bottle of milk for Silva. I placed it next to her in case she woke up. I made my coffee and went to the balcony. I felt the morning breezes, breathed in the fresh air, and enjoyed the angelic voice of Fayrouz, who comforted my nerves.

I expected to be the only one up early. I'd forgotten the two lovers I often watched flirting on their balconies in the distance. The girl puts a notebook in front of her, and her eyes are on the young man walking to his balcony with a book in hand. His eyes watch the girl. She enters the kitchen, brings two cups of coffee back with her and invites him with shy gestures to have coffee. He gestures to her with his hand, telling her he wishes he could. He motions for her to drink both cups for him and her, then the young man puts on a mask, indicating that he's afraid of being infected by COVID. She leaves for a bit and returns with a mask. I watch this scene repeated every day in a slightly different way. They'd been meeting at a trash can under the guise of throwing out garbage. They stood at a distance. The Coronavirus does not distinguish between lovers and non-lovers.

Silva woke up and her yelling sounded as if she was quarreling with someone. I ran into the room and found her fighting with a cat that had entered through the window, snatched the bottle of milk, and was suckling it like a baby. Silva grabbed the bottle, but could not pry it from the cat. It jumped with the bottle to the window, but it hit the bars, and the bottle broke and milk spilled. The cat jumped outside. Her sad meow got louder. The saying goes: "The demon cat can always find the way out."

How many terrorists in this country come out of the eye of the needle, not from the window in front of everyone's eyes? Good and evil exist in all times and places and all beings. Yet some have no beauty within them, so their existence is a burden on society. It is difficult to see the difference between some people and wild beasts now. The only difference is in the different predatory methods. Sometimes you work hard raising a dog to ensure he remains loyal to you all his life, and he never forgets the bread you fed him. At the same time, some people eat and then spit in the pot you feed them from.

–

Silva was still asking about her father. She went to the street to wait. She saw the neighborhood children, who were older than her, playing in the street. She ran to play, but she sneezed. The children shouted: "Corona! Corona!"

The children ran from her quickly. She stood looking at me in silence. In her eyes, there was question and bewilderment. She didn't understand what was going on. She burst into tears. Back home, she grabbed the spare bottle of milk, then ran to the door and closed it. She was scared of the cat coming back again.

Those moments stirred memories. I imagined war scenes and kids running in panic after an explosion. Some ran toward the sound and damage instead of running away. Terror had crept into the minds and hearts of young children. Even a child's sneeze affected them.

At night, the light from the neighbor's window across from mine comforted me. The balcony of the house was the only outlet for Silva and me. My heart rejoiced when I saw the two lovers flirting, each of them on their balcony using sign language. On another day, though, the girl was alone and confused, missing the young man, as he did not come out to the balcony as usual. She was going in and out from her room to the balcony. Restless. Sometimes she'd use her cell phone and then throw it angrily on a small table on the balcony. The young man was not answering. I went inside. Later, the woman returned to the balcony. Her eyes watched for the young man. He still didn't appear.

The next morning, when I woke and went to my balcony she was still on her balcony. She hadn't slept.

Perhaps the painful question was still in her head: What happened to him?

She disappeared for a little time inside her room and returned. Hope is something a person cannot live without. Her eyes watched the young man's balcony. She was disappointed, so she entered her room and closed the door in exasperation.

The pandemic had destroyed so many customs and traditions, but it was unable to penetrate the hearts of two lovers. You didn't have to be in love with a person. You could love your country, your child, your father and mother. The important thing was that our heart beats with something called love.

***

CHAPTER 20

There were many questions I couldn't resolve, and they made me hesitate quite a bit. I asked myself, Why do we exist, and for whom?

Each of us has our special memories and then, in a short moment, they go with the wind.

When we think about our future, it's imaginary. Still, we are always searching after it among our current struggles. Being in this life for other's sake only serves to improve their lives. We forget ourselves, no matter how strong we are. We go through a time of weakness sometimes, swimming through emotions and thoughts, before rising again to find what we seek.

Maher's absence was my weakness. I couldn't find an answer to convince myself where he was and when he'd return. Yet I had to convince Silva. In this case, there must be a little white lie. I wished I could also believe it. I was feeling short of breath and I needed fresh air. I hoped Maher would come relieve me of the responsibility for his daughter that was starting to suffocate me.

My psychological comfort needed to come first. Anything or anyone that might harm me, even if I loved them, made me try to get away.

What made this confusing is that Maher's love had indeed entered my heart. Although extremely cautious of anyone arousing suspicion, I thought Maher could be the hero of my love story. In the coming days, though, this dream could become a nightmare.

Maybe he'd disappoint me and break my heart. I'd never met a man who lay in bed mourning a woman. He had always forgotten the woman with another woman. I had to be careful. Instead of chasing false love, I still had my entire life ahead of me.

Life is wide, but we narrow it by thinking our happiness is linked to certain things.

This happened to me. I was disheartened by Maher's absence. I became lazy, dependent, and waiting for him to save me from my circumstances, enriching my life beyond my cleaning other people's homes. I became isolated.

I needed to reconnect with people but I'd become reluctant to do so. This can be a natural reaction when someone finds themselves in danger. I had to remind myself I was not so weak. I wanted to prove I was different from my mother. I wanted to prove myself to those who had never forgotten my origin and held onto a negative opinion of me.

My mother refused to return to her homeland because of the gossip that consumed some people.

Drowsiness overcame me. As usual, before I fell asleep, I was on Facebook, searching for my mother because I didn't know what she looked like, thinking her image should be stored in my memory, but knowing only my thoughts took me to the happy ending drawn in my imagination.

In a dream, we spoke on the phone. We talked about the language of silence, understanding without words and through harbored pain and sadness, until I burst into tears. Her voice whispered in my ear for the first time. She apologized for abandoning me. She told me why she had left and justified the reasons. She advised me to take care of myself.

I didn't expect my reaction to be so extreme. I glowed like a fire and felt like a balloon that could not bear a pinprick. I couldn't control my temper, and my voice grew louder.

"Now you tell me to take care of myself?" I said. "I am no longer the child you left to suffer. You threw her out into the open, and left her to the wild beasts, while she was screaming and searching for a breast to feed her.

"You do not know how the word mother comes out of the mouth and through the lips, it sounds like mwah...a kiss. The kiss that I missed from you.

"Just like I missed the touch of tenderness when I got sick and spent the night tired and worrying while I was calling out to you.

"And like I missed sleeping in your arms while you stroked my hair. I am no longer the child Farah, who plays in the alley alone. The lonely outcast.

"I wished to live my childhood like the rest of the children, with my mother the one who wakes me up early, prepares a za'atar sandwich for me, puts it in my school bag, washes my face, combs my hair, and goes with me and my friends to school. You are the one who deprived me of living my childhood, which I lived in loss.

"I am so distracted by my thoughts that I can't defend myself. You have denied me of everything beautiful. Now I understand everything, everything people used to say about you, and how they looked at me sarcastically.

"I am Farah, who did not live happy days, only the clinking of pots can preserve my dignity and keep me alive with hope. With all this, I have never forgotten you as you have forgotten me.

"The Lord has not forgotten me. He sent Um Bassam, who raised me, worked hard for me, and taught me without a school. I am not entitled to enter schools because I am of unknown parentage. After losing Um Bassam, I became homeless. I enter houses I don't know to live now. Yet she is the one who deserves the word 'Mother.' Not you. I will never forgive you!

She screamed in a voice that almost ruptured my eardrum.

"Farah, let me speak. I never forgot you. I was always waiting for your news. I checked on you while you were in Um Bassam's house. I knew her very well. She was the woman who I trusted sincerely."

I interrupted.

"Motherhood is a message and you did not complete it," I said. "The mother is not the one who gives birth to a child and throws it on the street. The mother is the one who raises, teaches, suffers, sacrifices, and stays up late. My dream has always been to see you or talk to you and hug you until now. That was when I was young and justified what you did because I didn't know what your circumstances were, except from what people would say.

"But now I will not forgive you. I will not forgive you. I will not forgive you! Now, I'm not the nameless little girl. I am Farah who was miserable and tired and endured. And entered people's homes to work and bear their orders for the sake of a decent living. I met many weak souls who tried to take advantage of me.

"Working as a maid was like a school that gave me important lessons. I learned a lot through my interactions with all kinds of people.

"I am now Farah, who is still looking for joy and making her wishes come true."

Due to my extreme agitation, I stuttered. My mouth went dry and my teeth clenched in frustration. I had a hard time swallowing.

In the dream, I tossed in my bed and the phone fell from my hand. After finding it, I tried to keep talking to my mother. "Hello, hello, hello."

She did not respond. I threw it as hard as I could against the wall, and I woke up when it shattered and landed in pieces on the floor.

Silva also woke up, screaming and uncertain about what was happening. I took Silva to the balcony of the house. I drank coffee to wake up. It was my only outlet. The nightmare would trouble me, the rest of the day.

Still, I heard sounds of congratulations and joy occasionally. My neighbor, the woman from the balcony across the way, looked down the street with a smile and waved her hand happily. I thought she'd seen the young man, the one she could always be comfortable with without speaking.

I eventually found out through his family that the young man had been infected with Coronavirus. He was in quarantine until recovering.

Immediately after returning he went onto the balcony and looked for his neighbor. She was waiting, expecting him to come see her.

She looked at him silently, and he also looked at her expressing his longing to actually meet her. The emotional silence between them was strong.

When parents are stingy in expressing their emotions of love for children, their offspring grow up to be poor at expressing their feelings, too. Much remains secret because they are not used to expressing feelings promptly.

It wasn't only me who endured emotional silence as a result of losing my mother and father. Some endure it even though they live in the arms of their families.

***

CHAPTER 21

Farah felt uneasy when she called Maher's sister to check on him, but she explained that Maher didn't tell her where he was. His sister shocked Farah by saying he'd left in the middle of the night to help put out a fire in an olive grove he owned on the coast and died in the rescue mission. Although he'd moved hundreds of kilometers away from the Syrian coast, his native land was something he'd wanted to hold onto.

"Oh Farah, he told me he didn't tell you about his urgent travel fearing you would worry about him," she said.

Maher's sister said he was always saying how happy he was to have met Farah and about the love she gave to Silva. Maher even told his sister he was planning to ask for Farah's hand during the olive harvest season.

The call ended with us both crying, and his sister planning to come get Silva. I won't pretend—I was hurting terribly after parting with Silva. With her, I'd learned the meaning of motherhood, which lies in raising and nurturing rather than only giving birth. She clung to my clothes, refusing to go with her aunt. I still heard her voice talking to her toys, her happiness dancing before my eyes. She still felt part of me. I had no choice but to leave the house filled with negative energy that darkened my eyes.

I still have not stopped crying over Silva's parting.

Aunt Um Saleh was one person I knew who could help ease my burdens. She felt bad for not having me visit sooner.

"I missed you so much, too" I said, "but circumstances kept me away from you."

"Is your distance from me because of corona, Farah?" she asked. "Your aunt, Um Saleh, was not afraid of the Coronavirus and does not take the virus seriously. We believe in our faith and what was written for us by God of a predetermined life and distributed sustenance, Oh Farah. I thought you had gone somewhere else."

"Where will I go, Um Saleh, in search of a town of calm and safety?" I said. "I still have not found it."

I told her I was taking care of a newborn whose mother died in labor and no longer had to work in people's homes. I told her about Maher's death.

"Oh, Farah," Um Saleh said. "This war has burnt trees, and deprived their owners of their source of income. Along with wasting their labor, sweat, and hope for their livelihood."

Um Saleh wondered how I would make a living now. I told her I was looking for work until I passed the high school exams and entered university.

"Pray for me to get the marks that qualify me to study law," I said.

"May the Lord grant you success," she said. "I will give you the address of a family that needs someone to work."

"Now tell me about you, Um Saleh. I remember the beautiful evening when you formed the virtual government."

"The new government has made things worse, and now we are missing the past. I am not the same as I used to be, Farah. I have become too old, and the social activities are not right for me anymore. I will tell you what happened to me.

"I visited a friend of mine in the neighborhood, and when I left her house to return, I became dizzy, and I lost my way. I turned around, spinning without being guided, and the sun was about to set. I felt like I had lost my memory as if I was seeing the neighborhood for the first time. I met the neighbors, but I was ashamed to ask them: Where is my home? I stood a while hoping maybe I would remember. At this moment I was afraid that I had completely lost my memory. Then, our neighbor approached, looking at me, surprised at my bewilderment.

"He seemed to have noticed my hesitation. He greeted me and asked, 'Are you looking for something that you have lost, Um Saleh?' I replied: 'No, never.' I did not tell him my head was spinning, and that I did not know the way. I answered him arrogantly: 'I like to go for walks.'

"I continued walking, but my head was still spinning badly. I saw neighborhood boys on the playground. I felt that I had woken up from my dizziness when I saw the children in the neighborhood, yet I asked one to walk with me so I wouldn't return home alone.

"I sat amazed at what happened to me, knowing everyone I saw on my way. I just lost my sense of direction. I was afraid that what happened to me was the beginning of Alzheimer's disease.

"The story did not end here, Farah. The next day some neighbors visited me to check on me. They had heard I completely lost my memory. They did not believe it since from that moment on I was fully conscious as if nothing happened. It was surprising that the neighbors talked about my condition and added more spice to it."

"God bless you, Aunt Um Saleh," I said. "The important thing is that you should not go out alone anymore. I will go with you wherever you want. If you'd known what happened with me, you wouldn't believe it. I lost my eyeglasses a few days ago. I looked for them in the corners of the house. I didn't find them. I said to myself, 'Maybe they are in the closet. When I opened the closet, I saw myself in the mirror with my glasses on."

"You are still too young to forget," she said. "It seems the circumstances we are going through are the cause of everything that befalls us. Not just us but many. If you knew what worries I had, you'd be surprised. And with everything that happened, I still resisted, and made humor from a sad heart, so that I would not be a burden to others. I always strive to be accepted by society and to make my children happy after their father was martyred in the war. I always strive for them to be happy.

"My happiness was gone after my two young sons were martyred by terrorists. They set us back in everything, even in the thoughts of some people who don't fear the Lord. We are still patient with injustice, oppression, and destitution. Many young people emigrated. Our daughters became spinsters, and the white dress became a dream."

"It is getting late. I will bid you goodbye now, Um Saleh."

The memories returned and took hold of me more, as I neared my house. Yet I worried. How can I live without Silva? This house is now empty of everything beautiful, I thought.

The cat greeted me outside meowing. She seemed hungry, and, as I hurried in, she scurried into the house ahead of me. She found the empty bottle of milk and brought it to me. Then she went looking for something else. She went into the kitchen and brought another bottle of milk that I used for Silva. She played with it as if asking me about Silva. She was missing her, too. I imagined Silva in the room, her toys still scattered. I imagined her petting the cat and arguing over the milk bottle.

The only time I had to study for the upcoming exam was at night, because during the day I'd returned to working in people's homes.

I needed to be very wary of this dreaded virus. As for the elderly, life had lost purpose for some because of fear and risk. They waited for the end of their lives. As for the smallest children, our angels, they became an obsession for adults, who fear their infection. We began to receive death without weeping, to mourn our dead without consolation, to bury our dead without prayer. The end of life was only a matter of time. All these dark fears and thoughts were unforgettable.

Before I fell asleep, I remembered my mother and hoped I would find her in my dreams. That would make my day happy. I knew now she never thought of returning to the country. Yet even in her absence, those who knew her story have not forgotten her. One saying goes, "The parents eat the unripe grapes, and the children suffer of the sourness and pay the heavy price."

The following day, I went to the house Um Saleh told me about. They appeared to be very wealthy before I knew anything about their lives. But from their loud voices and discussions, the constant anger and nervousness on the mother's face, it became clear there were problems.

I finished my work every day in silence. I was afraid to ask the homeowner any questions because the response would be harsh. This was how she spoke to one of her daughters who was about 20. The entire family looked at that girl differently. She was the only one whose name I knew from so many shouts.

"Salwa, go to the bathroom," they screamed.

I was surprised by the awful way they treated Salwa. Their daughter seemed like a stranger. She was a student at the university, though. I wondered what mistake she'd made to be punished by everyone. One day I met the beautiful, kind Salwa, who stayed isolated in her room. Salwa was always studying while the noise of her sisters' banter and laughter echoed through the home. Her mother sometimes shouted at Salwa, "Get into your room!"

I was surprised when Salwa called me over while her mother wasn't around. She whispered in my ear, "Oh, Farah, when you enter to tidy my room, make everything beautiful and clean in it. Let my room be like my sisters' room."

I was amazed she didn't know I would take great care being new to their house. After I finished cleaning her sisters' bedrooms, I entered Salwa's bedroom. Her room didn't fit in this palace. Everything seemed different. Salwa's bed was covered with nylon and had a stench. I wore a mask, but smelled it from afar. I opened the window and took everything in the room to the balcony. Fortunately, the scorching sunlight of a summer's day would sterilize her things. I went to the kitchen to finish my work there, waiting until the mattress dried and the odor dissipated. Um Salwa was making coffee in the kitchen and noticed me trying to remove the filthy stink on my clothes.

"I do not want anyone to know about Salwa," she said.

"What do you mean?" I asked.

She told me Salwa had a bedwetting problem since birth. I kept quiet. I didn't answer, still in shock by everyone's treatment of Salwa. I understood I had no right to argue with her mother. I feared saying any hurtful word. I continued completing my work in silence, but I was thinking about beautiful, young Salwa.

I wondered: How will she continue in this house? She is like a stranger and besieged by their sarcastic looks. Does she not have the right to receive care and kind treatment from them? She could overcome her ordeal and heal, and not be made to feel inferior, weak, and humiliated.

I decided not to continue working in their house. I couldn't bear watching what happened every day without interfering. I had to leave this house. In spite of possessing wealth, it lacked joy.

I'd hoped to see Salwa when she came home and saw her room. She'd be happy, and I could share her joy. Yet I didn't want to hurt her feelings about leaving.

Outside, the sky was clear and the sun was high, the gentle spring breeze smelled like flowers that could refresh melancholy hearts.

A job ad caught my eye in a storefront displaying beautiful party dresses. The store was looking for a young woman to hire. I entered without hesitation. The shop owner sat on a broad chair behind a Beech wood table, a cigarette with a golden filter in his mouth.

"Welcome!" he said, along with an exhale of smoke.

After I said I'd seen the ad, he straightened his seat and stared at me. He started asking me questions. I told him my mother and family were all lost in the war. He shook his head, as he was not satisfied. He asked for my ID card. I said my name on the ID was not what people called me.

"Everyone knows me as Farah. Rayan is my legal name."

"Why don't you like the name Rayan? Who chose the name Farah?"

"My mother had chosen it for me. When I was three years old, I did not answer anyone calling me, 'Rayan!'

I called myself Farah because I loved this name. It was enough that I could not choose anything in my life, is it not my right to choose a name I like?"

He stared at me again from head to toe, without saying anything. From his gaze, I felt unwanted. I stood waiting to hear him say yes or no. He shook his head to break the silence.

"Come back tomorrow, maybe it will be good."

I arrived home and started trying on clothes to wear. I didn't find any of them suitable, as some were torn and others weren't my size.

I began to think the way he looked at me was saying my worn-out clothes weren't appropriate to work in his luxurious place. I lay in bed thinking how I might be able to buy new clothes. I felt inspired to write whatever was on my mind:

The night is long but in my soul, a light conquers the darkness.

The parting of the soul is also prolonged, and in my heart are the flames of longing.

Silence prolongs, and my thoughts clash with difficult questions.

Illness prolongs, but we have patience.

The blockade is prolonged, but our strong fist breaks its heavy locks.

The war is prolonged, but we are waiting for peace.

Too much to say, and there is no point in screaming in this deaf world.

I will not stop looking for my mother even if that takes too long. She is the one who will illuminate the darkness of my night, extinguish the flames of my longing, answer my difficult questions, and ease my pain. She is my peace, and then the talk ends.

–

I turned to open my novel. It led me to another world in which I could swim in its space and learn about new cultures, customs, temperaments, and experiences.

I hurried and prepared a cup of tea to help me focus. I continued reading because of the sincerity I sensed in my book. It was about spontaneous actions without complicating matters. The writer was not interested in outdated habits. He was completely convinced that when we are honest with our feelings, and express what is inside us without ambiguity the result is always good.

I often stayed awake late so I'd become very sleepy. I wanted to move away from the bitter reality imposed on me. Still, I had nightmares. And I woke up every day with the same questions: Why was I created on the sidelines of life? How can I change people's views about a sin committed by my mother?

I wanted to enter the university and draw my future with my own hands. I was tired of cleaning people's homes. I barely had time for breakfast before returning to the shop where I was promised work. I wondered if he'd accept me for the job or sneer at my clothes.

***

CHAPTER 22

I was on my way to the dress shop, hoping for a new job. I imagined it would be better than domestic work. My imagination wandered into the beautiful nature surrounding me. The trees lined the roadside and the birds moved to and from with so many different chirps, languages that meant so much to them. It sounded like they were checking on something.

Perhaps one was checking on its babies, another on his mother, and another looking for its mate. One bird, perhaps preoccupied with the future of its young flies to the top of the tree to build a nest to keep them safe. It is like they are on a battlefield but one with overwhelming love. I wish all battles were like this.

At the shop, I became hesitant when I saw the employees all pristinely dressed and adorned. I asked one woman about the employer, and she looked me over.

"Are you the one cleaning the shop?" she asked.

"No, I'd like to work with you as a saleswoman."

She said he'd arrive soon and I should wait. My eyes landed on the beautiful clothing on display, wishing I could buy an outfit. Unfortunately, the prices didn't match my income.

The shop owner entered while I stood in front of a dress I liked very much, with its heavenly blue color and beautiful style.

He smiled. I quickly cast my gaze to the ground sheepishly. I knew if I wore this dress, it wouldn't change who I was. Instead, whoever knew me would whisper, "Where did she get this from? We know her as a housekeeper."

The owner sat behind his wooden table before I approached.

"Do you like the blue dress, Farah?" he asked.

I hesitated before answering.

"Yes, I like the shop and the dresses!"

And then the real questions began.

"Do you like this profession and how long have you worked in it? Do you have the ability to deal with customers?"

"I have never worked in this profession. Inshallah, I can meet your expectations with customers."

"You know there are only a few days left this year, you are welcome in the New Year."

–

I went home and waited until evening for my private tutoring session. Another woman waiting for a session with the teacher was the daughter of a wealthy family whom I'd worked for.

"I know you," she said with a rude tone. "You are the maid who worked in our house, I knew you from your clothes. You are still wearing the same clothes."

She watched my lesson, and when she saw me responding to the teacher, she began to make up words out of jealousy, confusion, and sarcasm. The teacher was trying to stop her. Yet she didn't stop talking, boasting, and showing off, saying she didn't wear clothes from the manufacturers of her country. Even her shoes were imported, she said.

I didn't care about what she said, because everyone knew her father accumulated his wealth by smuggling.

As I expected, this girl's performance in her session was poor, with the teacher reminding her of the prior lesson continually. She didn't answer anything. She cared little about studying. Her anger worsened when she heard my correct answers to the teacher's questions, and she looked at me with anger, seeking to quarrel.

The teacher sensed this and began to encourage her to pay attention to her studies.

"Don't be afraid," the teacher said. "You can enter the program of study you want."

She answered insolently that she could do anything with her father's money, and said she was the only heir to her parents' fortune. She looked at me with anger still, then she said to the teacher.

"From now on, I will not sit with a maid behind a common table. Her social class does not allow her to take a lesson with me."

I could no longer bear her meanness. I was very angry, but before I uttered a word she pulled my hair, ripping a lock from its roots. It hurt badly, but I managed to slip away. As for the teacher, he watched in fear, knowing she was paying him a lot of money for lessons. She did whatever she wanted with her father's money. No one held her father accountable either. Nobody asked: Where did you get this from?

I picked up my notebooks and never returned, not wanting to encounter a person like that again. Although I was used to enduring hurtful words from callous people, I decided to try to forget that silly event when I passed the shrine of one of God's saints. I entered the yard out of curiosity. Each family in the yard formed a circle. Some were eating and some drinking. Several doors opened to rooms full of visitors. Anyone who climbed the stairs into this building entered a slightly distinct room off these little rooms. The room felt sacred.

My turn came and I entered to see what was happening in the other room. It was crowded with people circling the shrine and kissing its stones in reverence. Verses were written on some stones. People whispered supplications for what they lacked. I leaned against the wall near the door, listening to what others said in faint voices.

Most asked forgiveness for mistakes. Some asked God to bless them with money so they could continue living with their children.

Some asked to be cured of illness.

Some prayed for the crisis to end in Syria, bringing an end to compulsory military service for children.

Some asked for the return of all those displaced from their country.

Some asked for a son or a daughter. Either one.

Another in a wheelchair, asked for wellness and good health.

A very elegant young man prayed by saying he lacked nothing of luxury but lacked a happy home life.

I was surprised at this and everything I saw. For the first time, I'd entered a shrine of a saint. I asked myself: Would the wishes of these people be fulfilled? Why did I remain a spectator knowing I could kiss stones like them?

Every day thousands of people kiss the same stones. The Coronavirus was still killing people, but they didn't care at all. Did they know something I didn't? Or did they not know anything?

I desperately needed to pray to meet my mother, who remained my obsession. She was present in the air I breathed. From that knowledge, I am refreshed and my hope is renewed.

I wondered if our prayers were accepted without kissing stones. Why were people accustomed to imitating each other when searching for the truth? The answer will always be: "It's a tradition, our ancestors used to do this."

Hence, many are lost between the past and present.

At the same moment, Silva, the beautiful child, crossed my mind. I would've liked those beautiful days to continue, but fate has no mercy. Since the day she left my house for her aunt's house, I'd been trying to talk to her on the phone. Her aunt hadn't answered me. I didn't know why but many circumstances and surprises are to be expected.

I asked the Lord to have Silva again one day. We were bound by a common destiny and a longing for a mother. All I asked while sitting next to the shrine of the saint was that this wish be fulfilled.

I was thinking in meditation, as if a videotape of my mother was playing for me. Although she lived in another country, I felt like she was next to me. I was living with her. She was apologizing for leaving me, and I was listening to her justifying why she left me with nothing. She explained several reasons for leaving me. She asked me to forgive. I forgave her.

But soon I was driven by torment and people's words that resounded in my ears, holding me responsible for what she'd done wrong. I screamed at her loudly.

"Why haven't you asked about me yet?"

I imagined her speaking to me regretfully.

"I will never forget you, Oh Farah, and I still regret what I did to you, my conscience reprimands me, I always think of you, and I am worried about you because of the deviants of society, who do not fear God. I moved away to the end of the world to forget what I did, but I was surprised when I met women from the Syrian community in Berlin who knew me before. They looked at each other and whispered in each other's ears. I could hear what one woman was saying to another: 'Don't you know her? She is Fuda the daughter of the chicken seller Abu Riyad, who did something shameful and ran away from her parents' house.' How big this world is, and how small it is at the same time."

The dream tape repeats in my memory. I told myself: I began contemplating beautiful things, but the subconscious mind would not stop remembering what fate had made for me against my will. I turned my eyes to the setting sun, its rays now hiding behind distant hills. I returned to my house thinking my hope might possibly shine again tomorrow with sunrise.

No wish was fulfilled, though, even the door of the shop where I was promised a job was closed the next day.

No matter how many doors closed on me, I would continue to ignite the lights within me, until hope came. The hope I lived in my dreams and waking life

*

GLOSSARY

Darbaka: An hourglass-shaped hand drum having a single drumhead, typically held in the lap or under the arm. It is widely used in Middle Eastern music.

Hookah: A tobacco pipe of Near Eastern origin with a long, flexible tube by which the smoke is drawn through a jar of water and thus cooled

Ghazlani: Sleeping with half-closed eyes like the gazelle.

Za'atar: A Middle Eastern spice blend made usually of dried herbs (such as thyme or marjoram), dried sumac, and sesame seeds.

Azrael: The angel of death in Jewish and Islamic thought who watches over the dying and separates the soul from the body.

Um: Prefix commonly used meaning "mother of".

Abu: Prefix commonly used meaning "father of".

Babur Gas: (Primus stove) is a portable pressure-burner stove fueled by kerosene or white gasoline, known for its reliability and use in various types of expeditions for cooking and heating.

Caesar Act: A United States legislation that sanctions the Syrian government, including Syrian President Bashar al-Assad, for war crimes against the Syrian population. President Trump signed The Act into law in December 2019 and it came into force on June 17, 2020.

Flag Service: An official banner authorized by the military service for families who have members serving in the Syrian Military.

Samira Tawfiq: (born 1935) was an iconic Arabic singer and actress active in the years 1948 - 1995. She became famous for her Bedouin style of singing.

Pullman: Large luxury bus with a refreshment facility.

Force majeure: Is a common clause in contracts that essentially frees both parties from liability or obligation when an extraordinary event or circumstance beyond the control of the parties, such as a war, strike, riot, crime, epidemic, or sudden legal change prevents one or both parties from fulfilling their obligations under the contract.

Fayrouz: She is considered by many as one of the leading vocalists and most famous singers in the history of the Arab world. Fairuz's fame spread in the 1950s and 1960s, leading her to perform in various Arab capitals, including Damascus, Amman, Cairo, Rabat, Algiers, and Tunis.

Inshallah: "if God wills" or "God willing".

Shahba: Is a city in Syria located 87 km (54 mi) south of Damascus.

KHAYAT